Praise for the w

Tak

Abbott has skillfully portrayed the characters in this tale. A bit of a "cozy" with a little "thriller" thrown in for good measure, the story makes us feel as if we're walking alongside CJ and Alex, discovering answers and experiencing how each revelation affects them. This story is an easy read—delightfully entertaining, jam-packed with baffling suspects and a surprising twist, all leading us to its satisfying end. A great read for the couch or the beach.

-*Lambda Literary Review*

I enjoyed getting to know more background on CJ. These books are mystery romances, but they still have enough excitement to keep you on your toes. Technically, this book could be read alone, since the crime solves itself in one book. But if this is the first Alex and CJ book you have read, you would be missing out on so much. Especially the chemistry that brought these two together.

-Lex Kent's Reviews, *goodreads*

Erica Abbott's writing is great as usual with all literary elements done well. The plot is strong and very interesting with a dominating mystery-solving part which holds one's interest all through. *Taken In* is a delight to read as well as the rest of this series and I recommend it heartily.

-Pin's Reviews, *goodreads*

Desert Places

Ms Abbott uses her native Colorado to great effect with stunning scenery, moonlight walks and sunset rides. The love of place is evident and adds a depth to the story, where the Hawkins are firmly rooted in the land and the community. Good

storytelling, likeable characters and a charming romance...
I thoroughly enjoyed this, a light and fast read, perfect for a
summers day in the garden.

-Lesbian Reading Room

One Fine Day

One Fine Day: Brainy is the new sexy! A complex and mature
romance where everyone has a bit of history, *One Fine Day*
intersects professions of corporate law and the world of opera,
while commenting on the impact of homophobia in both.
Abbott's characters are vivid. Most are smart, well-rounded,
interesting, and often funny...

-Lambda Literary Review

Praise for the work of Pol Robinson

Open Water

Open Water is a well-told tale of the triumph of human emotion in the face of adversity. In addition, it's an excellent love story told against a backdrop of Olympian proportions. This first offering from new author Pol Robinson could be a gold medal winner.

-Anna Furtado, *Just About Write*

Robinson has done her homework in giving descriptions of the boats and the technique it takes to bring them across the finish line. She also does a great job describing the scenes at Olympic village and the lives of the athletes. *Open Water* is an exciting read with just enough intrigue. It's also a good love story, told with humor and warmth.

-R Lynne, *Just About Write*

Open Water flows off of the pages. The story passes smoothly and quickly, almost emulating the strokes of the rowers' oars. The personality of each character contributes to the atmosphere of the book as well as the setting in Beijing. It's also a very clean book with no mistakes or misprints in it. That makes the reading even easier. If this is an example of what can be expected from Pol Robinson in the future, then readers have some good books to look forward to.

-*Piercing Fiction*

[Un]Common Ground

Other Bella Books by Erica Abbott

Desert Places
One Fine Day

The Alex Ryan and CJ St. Clair Series
Fragmentary Blue
Certain Dark Things
Acquainted with the Night
Taken In

Other Bella Books by Pol Robinson

Open Water

About the Author

Erica Abbott has been an attorney for nearly thirty years, many spent working with law enforcement and local government as a prosecutor. She has also taught legal courses, studied bridge and golf—mastering neither—and has appeared as a performer and singer in numerous local community theater productions in her beloved Denver, Colorado. She currently lives in Southern Colorado.

Publisher's Note:
Erica Abbott passed away on the 4th of July, 2020—just a few weeks before [Un]Common Ground was released. Writing this book with Polly, and seeing it published, meant the world to her and was truly a labor of love. It hurts knowing that she didn't get to hold it in her hands. But we are forever grateful for this one last gift from Erica. The loss is great.

About the Author

Pol Robinson is a professor, sometime sailor, and musician who thrives in the Pacific Northwest with her wife, a shared college kid, and two rescued dogs. When not doing something related to the above, you can find her in her shop, producing sawdust and the occasional bowl or vase. Pol's a past Goldie and Alice B. Reader award winner and is hard at work on her next book for Bella (or so she says).

[Un]Common Ground

Erica Abbott
and Pol Robinson

BELLA
BOOKS
2020

Bella Books, Inc.
P.O. Box 10543
Tallahassee, FL 32302

First Bella Books Edition 2020

Editor: Medora MacDougall
Cover Designer: Pol Robinson

ISBN: 978-1-64247-116-8

[Un]Common Ground

Erica Abbott
and Pol Robinson

BELLA
BOOKS
2020

Erica's Acknowledgment

This book was born from a late-night conversation at a Golden Crown Literary Society conference. Pol and I shared a room and started to discuss how opposites really attract. We each created a character and began to talk about what would happen if they fell in love. After many delays due to new jobs, relocation and health challenges, the resulting book is in your hands. It is unlike any book I have written before, and I could not have done it without Pol and our editor. I hope very much that you enjoy reading it as much as we enjoyed writing it.

Pol's Acknowledgment

As Erica wrote, the deep connections formed at the annual GCLS con provided the impetus for this book; this was our first venture into co-authoring and we're delighted to share with you our efforts. Many thanks to Erica (and K) for juggling this project with other priorities, and the amazing Bella team: Jess, coordinator of all things, Ruth, the proofing goddess, the rest of the production peeps, and especially Medora MacDougall, editor extraordinaire, who smoothed the rough edges and soothed in order to do so. Last, but never least, endless thanks to the inestimable Linda Hill, who brings and holds us all together. We (speaking for Erica with permission) could never imagine writing with a better team.

Erica's Dedication

To love, always and forever.

Pol's Dedication

To Rebecca P., who was the very model of a modern major thespian; and to Erica Abbott, whose booming laugh knew no bounds, whose sharp wit and droll asides, delivered with a glint in her eye and a flash of a dimple, could (and would) reduce us to helpless laughter, often at inconvenient and/or inappropriate moments (which was, of course, her intent). The meat locker will never be the same without you.

PROLOGUE

She was coming home.

The wide-open mouth of the ferry offered a panoramic view of the slowly approaching islands, as well as the perfect scoop for the ever-present winds that rose with the evening sky. Powerful enough to knock a person down, the wind reached only so far, almost seeming to form a semi-solid, invisible wall. Standing tucked inside that wind-wall, close enough to feel it but not be suffocated by it, Sara tucked her hands in her pockets and watched the sun set behind the snowcapped mountains of the Olympic Peninsula. Already the mountains and island before it were hulking black silhouettes against the painted sky. Red-gold fire limned the edges of clouds that laced the deepening-to-midnight blue of the sky beyond.

Sara took a long, deep breath in, savoring the salty tang of the Sound, colored by the faintest hint of evergreen and pine. Pitted and scraped white paint framed her view, the dings and dents of years of use added to the character of the MV Salish, the vessel churning its way across the Puget Sound. Hard concrete thrummed with the rhythm of the powerful engines, its surface stained with oil, old paint, and more scrapes that echoed those on the walls. This was always her favorite spot on the ferry, below-decks, away from the tourists counting jellyfish or snapping selfies against the backdrop of the worn and scraped ferry's pilothouse. Tucked just inside of the ramp area, legs braced against the gentle swell of Puget Sound, with just enough wind blowing in to lift her long, brown hair from her neck.

Home.

It had been three years this time.

Of the many places her parents had ever called "home"—and there had been many in their 30-year sojourn with the Peace Corps—this one was the one that meant the most. Tucked deep into the towering pines and birches of Vashon Island, the little house her parents found when they retired nearly seven years ago, with its small rooms and creaky old floors had grabbed her from the first moment she had seen it.

Sarasvati Noelani Chandler was coming home.

And this time, she was home to stay.

* * *

"What do you mean, 'we're moving'?" Sara stared at her mother, dumbfounded. In fact, thinking about it, Sara realized her dad had not said much of anything about himself or her mother, instead adroitly turning the conversation back to Sara and her work with Home Grown International for the last three years and her new move to Grassroots Gardens' local satellite agency, Community Gardens of Seattle. Not until they had rolled into the driveway had her dad even hinted at any changes. She stood in the doorway, her bag at her feet, and simply stared at her mother. The living room was a jumble of boxes and stacks of books. Pale green walls accented with photographs and drawings collected by the three of them for years still lined the walls, with a gap or two here and there. In the midst of all of this stood her mother, stacks of brown paper at her feet, a cluster of glasses and plates stacked on the small table beside her.

At barely five feet, Sandy Chandler provided a counterpoint to her husband's six-and-a-half-foot frame. Everything about her was petite, save for her voice. She could boom out a laugh that rivaled that of her husband, Bill. Both lived life to the fullest, and Sara loved everything about them. Her dad nudged her inside and Sara stepped further into the house and hugged her mother. "*Baba*," she said, falling back into her use of the Nepali term of endearment automatically, "didn't say anything about moving when he picked me up!"

"Oh, he didn't, hmm?" Sandy Chandler gave her daughter a final squeeze and a smile as she stepped back and began to wrap another glass in brown paper. "I'm sure he was too excited about seeing you to think of it."

"*Aama*," Sara took the wrapping paper from her mother's hand and pulled her to the old couch, pushing aside boxes to make room, "what's going on?" Looking around, she slid her free hand through her hair in frustration. She had been so looking forward to coming home, to be again in a place where she belonged. Where she fit. And once again, she was being uprooted. "I thought you were happy here, working on the preserve."

After more than thirty years as RPCVs, Returning Peace Corps Volunteers, Bill and Sandy Chandler had turned in their badges, their well-worn duffels, and settled on Vashon Island. That had been almost seven years ago. They'd purchased their first-ever actual house, so different from the weatherworn scraps of wood with a thatched roof that had been gifted to them by the elders of the tiny village in which she'd been born. Her parents had moved here, made friends in the community, and settled in. For good, it had seemed to Sara, and she had been glad. They weren't getting any younger and she had been happy to think of them settled here on the island. Still doing good works, but in a more stable and safer place. Their being happy here had been a driving factor in her own recent change of plans and of jobs. *Well*, she admitted to herself, *one of the reasons*.

Sandy leaned back into the cushions, their worn fabric covered by a quilt nearly as old as the couch, and smiled up at her daughter. "You haven't called me '*Aama*' in a while, Sara-*ji*."

"Why so formal, *Aama*?" Growing up in Nepal, Sara knew the ins and outs of Nepali better than she did English. Her mother's addition of the "ji" to her name was only done in formal address, and she had rarely heard it from either of her parents. She sat up in sudden panic and gripped her mom's fingers. "You're not sick, are you? What about *Baba*?"

"No, honey. We're fine. Relax." Sandy pulled her daughter back until Sara was slumped against her. She tucked Sara's hand in hers and leaned her head against her daughter's shoulder. "It's *so* good to have you home. No, *Baba* and I are fine. We're just… well…" Sandy trailed off and sighed.

"Bored." Bill's booming voice filled the room. "By god, Sara, we're bored out of our ever-lovin' minds here." He sat on the arm of the couch and took Sara's other hand. "Your *Aama*'s embarrassed to admit it, but we made a mistake."

Sara tipped her head back and studied her dad, his wide-set eyes in a face seamed with wrinkles created by a combination of a life lived outdoors and his ready smile. A square, stubborn jaw, something he had passed down to his only child, though thankfully hers had been softened by Sandy's touch, was as ruddy as the rest of his skin and covered in a stubborn silver stubble even this early in the day. His hair, once a midnight black was now a fabulous nimbus of silver-gilt, a color echoed in the large, bushy eyebrows he now raised at her scrutiny.

"You're not seriously thinking of going back to the Peace Corps, are you?" She looked from one parent to another, her heart thumping.

"No, we have something else in mind, *sānō chōrī*."

"*Baba*, I have not been your 'little daughter' for years." Sara narrowed her gaze. "Out with it."

"Busted." Bill chuckled and winked at Sandy before shrugging. "No, the Peace Corps is a game for your generation now. We're bored, not insane. And," he cupped her chin, "you have to be much older than twenty-eight to no longer be my *sānō chōrī*." Bill shrugged and stretched. "No, we've got something else planned."

Bill pulled Sara up and into his arms, his usually loud voice muffled by his bulk as she was buried against his chest, her face pressed into the nubby worn cotton of his sweatshirt. She closed her eyes and breathed in the warm, cottony scent of him overlaid with the tang of wood smoke and a hint of sawdust. "We're not going all that far away, honey. Just over to Whidbey Island. They were looking for a new sanctuary caretaker and someone to head up the educational outreach program, so we applied." He squeezed her again and released her with a smacking kiss on her cheek. "Can you believe it? They took us!"

"But," Sara looked around the living room, still cozy despite the piles of already packed boxes. "This is *home*, you love this place." She hesitated, then added, "You've only been here for seven years. And..." she paused again, her voice catching slightly. "It's the first time we've had a real home in...well, forever."

"You know that home is—"

"Yes, I know." Sara blew out a breath and repeated the words she'd heard throughout her childhood. "'Where those we love reside.' I get it. I do. But..." She shrugged. "I love this place. I thought that, you know, for once, we would have a real...home. Together."

"And," Bill added as he slid off the arm of the couch, pulling her with him to sit between Sandy and himself, "since they have a really nice caretaker's cottage over there, we thought you might want to just live here."

"It's the perfect solution for everyone, Sara. You love this house, we knew that, so...now you have it all to yourself! The timing works well too! You have six weeks to get settled before you start at Community Gardens, and Baba and I have a month to get settled in the new place." Sandy's brown eyes were wide and entreating, clearly hoping Sara would agree with them.

Their enthusiasm was hard to resist, and Sara could see how happy and excited they were. She gave them a smile that she hoped wasn't as weak as she feared, settling back into her dad's embrace, as her mom began to tell her about their newest plans for adventure, her dad providing the color commentary as needed.

She had wanted to come *home*, not just to a place, but to them. *They* were her home, her place, her grounding. She had allowed herself to believe that she could come here, to them, to this place, and they would somehow make it right again. Make *her* right again. Nothing was right, inside. Everything felt upside-down. Had felt that way since Devery. Since walking in and having her say, in her stumbling, halting way, that she wanted Sara gone. That she wanted Sara to go. *Needed* Sara to go.

So she had gone. Run, even. With barely more than the clothes on her back, a few items from her room, and a worn canvas backpack. She had gone directly to the airport—or as directly as you could when you started from the ass end of nowhere. She had come here this time to stay, to spend time with them again, something she had missed since they'd retired and she had continued to travel. She needed that anchor after everything fell apart in the last few months. And with that anchor pulling up, she was adrift again.

CHAPTER ONE

"Watch out!"

The car stopped inches away from Margaret's thigh, brakes squealing in protest. She waved a hand at the driver, half in apology and half in dismissal as he cursed her clearly and colorfully from within the safe confines of his sedan.

Margaret continued to jaywalk across the lanes of the downtown street with her other hand adjusting the Bluetooth device in her ear.

"I am thirty-seven years old and I do not need for my *mother* to get me dates!" Margaret said in exasperation.

"I know how old you are, dear. I was there when you were born." Her mother's serene voice irritated Margaret even more. "Now honestly, how long has it been since you had a nice dinner with some lovely woman?"

Margaret hopped over the curb, balancing perfectly on the sidewalk in her designer stilettos. She loved the sharp sounds the heels made on the concrete as she walked. The heels made her taller than most other people on the street and she liked that too.

"I had lunch last week with Bobbie," Margaret said, trying to keep the pout out of her voice.

"Ex-girlfriends do not count."

"Why not?"

Her mother cleared her throat delicately. "We are looking for long-term relationship material here. Someone you want to come home to instead of working all the time."

Margaret dodged three men with briefcases moving like a phalanx down the middle of the crowded early morning sidewalk. She threw them a withering glare and said, "You mean someone to give you grandchildren, don't you?"

"That would be nice, too." Her mother sounded wistful now. Not for the first time, Margaret wished she had had a sibling or two to divert her mother's relentless attention from her own biological clock. Apparently, the kids produced by the five nanny goats her mother kept in the little upstate farm were not a sufficient outlet for her maternal instincts.

"I can find my own dates," Margaret repeated as she turned the corner. The City Annex building was halfway up the block. Once there, she could legitimately claim the priority of work to get out of this conversation.

"I know that you *can* find your own dates, Dusty. I just don't think you're making finding someone nice a proper priority."

"Don't call me Dusty, Mother. Look, I don't like blind dates. You don't even know this woman."

"Well no, but I've met her parents. Lovely people. They were very interested in my farm-made organic chèvres. Anyway, we were just chatting, and we discovered we both had single gay daughters, which just goes to show you how much the Universe conspires to…"

Flowers! She had forgotten the flowers, drat it. She needed to end this discussion and get back to her life. The life without a goat-cheese-creating-New-Age matchmaker interfering in it.

"Mom, I've got to go now. I'll call you tonight and you can resume rearranging my existence."

Margaret punched off the phone and slipped it into her Hermès bag. The flower shop was another block behind her, so she would have to hurry to get to work on time. On time, of course, meant before her assistant Jeremy arrived.

She thought about Jeremy as she marched back to the flower shop, not that she liked thinking about him. Jeremy was tall and good-looking. She could tell he was handsome because all the women in the office flipped their hair whenever he deigned to speak to them. Well, not all of them—Dee had really short hair and she ignored Jeremy whenever possible. Margaret suspected that Dee didn't date men, but she herself would never date anyone at work, so Dee wasn't an option.

The real reason she didn't like Jeremy is because she knew that he was after her job. She suspected that he was actively sabotaging her on occasion, but she hadn't been able to prove it yet. And she knew she would have to have rock-solid proof before her boss, the deputy mayor, would consider firing him.

Margaret smiled a moment as she entered the florist's shop, the little old-fashioned bell jangling above her. She liked the sound of it.

Billy looked up from the counter and grinned at her. "Thought you might have forgotten today, Ms. Winter."

"No, just a little late. Are they ready?"

He reached into the cooler for the arrangement, yellow daisies and red-striped carnations, and laid them gently in a tissue-lined white glossy box. "Every Friday, same flowers. Must be for somebody special," he said as he tied the box with a wide red satin ribbon, arranging the bow just-so until he was satisfied.

"It is. Just leave it on my account, Billy. Thanks again." She had her credit card on file with them. It saved time and she liked saving time.

"Sure thing," he called after her, but she was already through the door, the little bell's sound almost lost in the sounds of honking outside on the street.

In a moment of triumph, she got to her office to see that she had beaten Jeremy in again. Margaret chuckled to herself as she opened the door to her office, admiring as she did every weekday the neatly printed letters on the plaque beside the door: "S. Margaret Winter. Director of Neighborhood Development."

Not yet forty, and she had an important job in a big city. She had done a good job so far, and if the deal on her desk worked out, who knew how much further she might go?

She liked her office, tidy and yet filled with things that mattered. The most important was the big Seattle city map on the wall opposite the windows with the great view across the city. Lots of city officials wanted a bay view, but Margaret knew what mattered: buildings and the people who lived and worked in them. That was the city's life and future. People came for the scenery and the climate, but they stayed and paid taxes and contributed to the arts scene because the city was alive with other people doing the same things. People who needed jobs and places to live and create.

Margaret set her flowers carefully in an empty vase sitting ready at the corner of her desk, turning the vase so that the blooms faced the door, ready to capture the attention of anyone who came to see her. As she did each week, she just as carefully set aside the box they'd come in, so she could safely take them home this evening. Satisfied that all was as it should be, she hung up her suit jacket and began to tackle her voice mail and emails.

By the time Jeremy arrived at nine oh seven, officially seven minutes late, Margaret had already done more than an hour's work. Despite the early-morning phone call from her mother, the day was already going well. She was reviewing the report from the assistant who was in charge of the application process for the small business grants when a man's voice greeted her from the doorway.

"Good morning, Ms. Winter."

It was Jeremy, who was always annoyingly polite. She sat back from her desk and watched as he approached.

"Nice flowers," he remarked, as he did every Friday morning. Margaret admitted to herself that part of the reason she bought the flowers on the way to work rather than after was so Jeremy would wonder where they came from.

Jeremy had a face that started well from the top: wavy blond hair carefully styled to look casually surfer-boy, followed by a pair of nice sea-blue eyes. But things went downhill after that,

Margaret thought. His nose was a little too pug-like, and he had a weak chin, which he attempted to conceal with a carefully groomed goatee.

Actually, he looked a bit like one of her mother's goats, a crafty billy named Emmett. She grinned to herself, then quickly rearranged her face into boss mode.

"All right. Let's go over next week again."

He sat in her office chair, tugging his jacket down so he would sit on it and not let the fabric bunch up around his shoulders. His concession to casual Friday was to wear a navy blazer over light-colored slacks rather than a suit. Margaret, of course, did not believe in casual Fridays for herself. *Dress for the job you want*, she reminded herself, *not just the job you have*.

"You have a Chamber of Commerce breakfast at seven on Monday morning. The Planning Commission study session is Monday at one o'clock," Jeremy began, consulting his iPad. "They want an update on the C of C proposal for the University District project."

Margaret tapped her stylus on the stack of files on her desk. "Have we heard back from the merchant's association on The Ave?"

"Um, not the last time I looked." Jeremy looked a little flustered. Margaret loved asking him a question he hadn't anticipated. Point for her.

"Well, call what's-her-name over there and tell them if they have anything to add that they had better send me an email no later than noon Monday."

He made a note. "Beverly."

"What?"

"The head of The Ave's merchant's association. Beverly Morgan."

Margaret pursed her lips. His attempt to one-up her by remembering the woman's name didn't count—he had his contact list in front of him, so it wasn't that his memory was better than hers. No goal.

"And double-check the PowerPoint presentation before I get in front of the Planning Commission," she added. "You screwed it up last week."

He winced but made another note. "I'll make sure IT gets it right."

She leaned over her desk. "Check it yourself, too, Jeremy. We don't want to look like incompetents in front of the Planning Commission, do we?"

"No, ma'am. We don't." His tone was deferential, but he tugged at his goatee, a habit that Margaret interpreted as showing his nerves. She had made him nervous and flustered in one conversation. Game, set, and match to her. It was a good start to the morning.

They didn't really need to go over the calendar—Margaret was meticulous about entering all meetings and appointments into her phone. But three times in the last eight months Jeremy had "forgotten" to notify her of some change or addition and she wasn't going to let that happen again. The meeting shifted the blame for any problems with her schedule back onto him. Where she wanted it.

Lately he had tried another tactic—the missing file. Even with the city's goal of the paperless office, there were lots of physical documents they needed: survey plats, maps, architectural blueprints, artists' renderings, mylars. Many were too large to fit in normal-sized file drawers, so Margaret had converted an old interior office into a file room for oversized documents—she hated clutter. But twice now she had asked for a document that couldn't be found when she needed it. As usual, she suspected Jeremy without being able to prove anything.

They finished the schedule review for the next week, then Margaret dismissed him with a list of tasks to be completed by the end of the day. She returned to her own list, barely interrupting her work for lunch. She sent Jeremy out for sushi from Sushi Cocina. This had the added advantage of sending him almost a mile away on foot. Too bad it wasn't raining.

Margaret saved her favorite project for a special Friday afternoon treat. She went down the hall to the interior file room and pulled her rolled-up map from the corner. Jeremy eyed her as she walked past his desk on the way back, and on impulse she made a detour.

"Did you check that PowerPoint yet?" she asked.

His eyes slid sideways. *Aha, got you,* she thought happily.

Behind him at a cluttered desk sat a woman Margaret didn't quite recognize. Her hair was as black as Margaret's own but in contrast to Margaret's smooth chignon, this woman had a mass of unruly curls. She looked up for a moment, met Margaret's gaze through huge tortoise-shell framed glasses, and quickly lowered her look to her messy desktop.

The glasses nudged her memory. Jeremy's intern from City College. Linda? Laura? Something. She returned her attention to Jeremy.

"Um, no, just getting to the PowerPoint." He tugged at his goatee.

She smiled sweetly. "Just shoot me a quick email when you finish looking it over," she directed, her tone now verging on the saccharine. *So I'll have a nice written record that you checked it in case anything goes wrong.*

"Of course, Ms. Winters."

Margaret trotted back to her office, humming cheerfully. She carefully closed the door behind her and then slipped the bands off the map and spread it across her conference table. Grabbing the flower vase, coffee cup, and pen holder from her desktop, she anchored the corners of the map.

There it was, her ticket up the political ladder. The new site for the international headquarters of Pacific Rim Robotics, located in downtown Seattle and bringing hundreds of jobs and millions of dollars to the local economy. Seattle was going to become more than just the home of coffeehouses and fish markets—this was the next big step to making her one of the great international cities of the world.

And Margaret was going to make it happen. She was determined to close this deal, and she got what she went after, always.

She ran a well-manicured fingertip around the block containing the three properties in question. The Sterne office property was already sewn up, in city ownership. The old Capital Hotel was under contract. It needed to be torn down anyway, so she was sure the closing wouldn't be a problem.

Pacific Rim had agreed, in principle, to a deal to lease the real property for their new headquarters from the city. The company would build the building, the city would reap the economic benefits, and Pacific Rim would eventually be able to buy the real estate from the city at a highly favorable price. *Win-win*, Margaret thought. She could already imagine herself standing next to the mayor at the press conference announcing the Pacific Rim deal, basking modestly in the glory of the biggest business coup for the city in years.

Her finger moved over an inch to the single impediment standing between her and that press conference: the Stockton Industries building. The negotiations were complicated, because the property was owned by the Stockton Family Trust, and dealing with a board of trustees was almost as bad as dealing with a city council. Stockton Industries could easily move their offices across the bay, where their warehousing and manufacturing operations were, but agreeing on the price was proving difficult. Still, Margaret was determined to make the project work. There was nowhere else in the city where Pacific Rim could get enough property to build their headquarters without spending more on the land than the building would be worth.

Jobs. Economy. And a faster track up in city government. She had to close the deal. Any way she could.

* * *

Margaret juggled her briefcase, purse, keys, and the flower box in two hands to unlock her condo door. She finally managed it and tumbled into her foyer.

Keys and briefcase went neatly on the small table that was there for that express purpose. The flowers she took to the kitchen where she popped them into the vase she had waiting on the large kitchen island. "Drink up, guys. One more stop to make." She strode directly across her living room, through the bedroom, and into her walk-in closet. The Hermès bag went into its designated cubby after she removed her wallet and phone. Shoes next, into their own shoe slot, heels out and exactly aligned to the sides.

She had spent some good money on installing a custom closet after she bought the condo a couple of years ago. Her suits and shoes and accessories were important parts of her look, which in turn was an important part of her career.

The condo itself was everything she wanted. It was downtown in a newly remodeled building with big windows and an art deco feel to the sculptured plaques on the exterior. Modern but not too hip: she didn't want to live with a bunch of partying twenty-somethings with jobs at downtown banks or law firms using family money to pay their condo fees. This building had older singles and couples, people like herself in mid-career or retired from professions that left them enough money for a boat or ski trips to Colorado in the winter. *Like dressing for the job you want,* Margaret thought, *you should live the life you aspire to have.* It took every penny she made, but the goal was what mattered.

Blouse into the dry-cleaning basket, suit carefully hung up. No wasabi or soy sauce drips from lunch, so it was good for another wearing or two. Bra next, with the concurrent sigh of relief. Sports bra, special wicking-material top, stretch capris, running shoes chosen to accommodate her over-pronating stride. Time for the treadmill in the workout room downstairs, then a few light reps with the free weights. Fridays were upper body day.

She got her water bottle from the refrigerator, pulled the bright flowers from the vase and, after shaking off the remaining water, placed them carefully back into the box before closing the lid and checking to be sure the ribbon was set just so. She grabbed her keys and the flowers and paced carefully, quietly to the elevator, checking the halls. No one there.

Now for the tricky part.

She rounded the corner and punched the elevator down button, trying to get her timing just right. When it was on its way up, she watched the floor indicator. It had taken her a few times to get it right, but she had it down now and so far she had never been caught.

When the indicator hit floor eight, Margaret scuttled away to the nearest unit, 1101. She placed the flowers carefully in front of the door, taking care to keep the box out of the traffic area of the hallway.

As she heard the elevator's soft ding, she scampered away, keeping her head below the level of the peephole of 1101 at all times. The elevator doors were open, just beginning to close, as she slid inside. She breathed a sigh of relief. Another clean getaway. Now time for a good end-of-the-week workout.

CHAPTER TWO

Sara dropped her keys onto her new desk and herself nearly as gracelessly into the chair behind it, barely avoiding sitting on the box of new business cards someone had left for her. What a month. Moving her parents to Whidbey Island and then helping them set up at the refuge had been more of an ordeal than she—or her parents, she would bet—had imagined. They weren't simply going out to count birds; it seemed they were responsible for the upkeep of the entire thing! She and her dad had made more trips to Home Depot in three weeks than she had done in her entire life before. Or at least it felt that way. When you added in the additional element of a ferry each time you had to take a trip…some of the charm of those ferry rides had begun to fade.

She had to admit, though, that once she had gotten over the initial shock, she found that she really loved living in the house alone. Okay, it had been a little creepy and odd the first night, and then the second, when whatever animal lived nearby decided to ramble across her porch, but all in all, she loved it.

Vashon Island was as serene and lush as she had remembered, and, for the first time in years, Sara woke to complete silence.

Okay, too much silence. She was seriously thinking of getting a dog.

Leaning back in her chair, she watched the shadows of the buildings creep toward her across Elliott Bay as the sun rose higher behind her. Ferries chugged their way to and fro, moving people from one island to the other, or to and from the mainland, in an endless back-and-forth that was as regular as the sunrise. Sara watched sailboats creep out of the bay and catch the wind, saw the cat-and-mouse of smaller watercraft darting between the larger commercial vessels. Her view was the source of endless entertainment, always the same dancers, but never the same dance. One of the best things she liked about working for the nonprofit Community Gardens of Seattle was her office. It was silly, she knew, to have based any part of her decision to leave Home Grown International, one of the largest global nonprofits focused on building and maintaining small, urban gardens for communities to sustain themselves, on what her office looked like, but Sara had to admit that it—and the view—had played a role.

Along with researching the Seattle arm of another nonprofit, she'd also chased off-the-record information, using the broad network of friends and coworkers she'd established while with HGI to learn that what she'd seen from the outside was a fairly accurate representation of what was on the inside: Community Gardens of Seattle operated as a semi-autonomous arm of Grassroots Gardens, allowing her and her colleagues a more hands-on approach to developing community-based gardening. They seemed to live their motto, *Growing Spaces, Building Community*, and had a strong reputation for building and sustaining honest, local community garden projects. Their primary goal was facilitating community-based gardens to combat the common urban "food desert," the difficulty low-income residents have in being able to buy affordable or good-quality fresh food.

Part of her research included what her dad had termed a good, old-fashioned "casing the joint," including projects the company had already completed and sites that might be suitable for future development of community-based gardens, and the minute she had seen the old industrial building on Seattle's west side, she had loved it. She had fallen deeper in love after being shown her own potential space during the tour following her interview. Whoever had led the renovation to convert the industrial space to business lofts had a heart for history. They had left the old iron framed nine-paned windows in place, even keeping the lower flip windows that allowed for ventilation. Exposed brick was accented by wood worn and scarred by time and use, and that wood ran across the ceilings and framed the large rectangular panes vertically set three-by-three into an iron grid. Those old grids formed large windows that made up the outer wall of her office. The restoration crew had even kept the original floors, simply smoothing and restaining them, the dark old wood still so solid after nearly ninety-five years that there was barely a creak in any part of her company's offices. Sara's office was enclosed, as were all of the others, with glass, allowing light to flow through the space with barely an interruption. One of the best parts about those glass walls, however, was a nifty trick her new assistant had shown her. With a flick of a switch, the glass turned opaque, a feature that was powered completely by solar panels. All in all, Sara thought as she leaned back in her chair and watched the morning sunlight dance on waves created by busy traffic on the bay, she much preferred this smaller, locally based company to HGI.

She opened the box of business cards and drew out a few to place in her wallet. Nice quality, she thought as she ran her finger gently over the surface. Recycled, heavy paper colored the palest green, the Community Gardens of Seattle logo set opposite her own name, her new title just below. *Sara N. Chandler, Executive Director*. Shaking her head, she tucked the cards she'd pulled out into her wallet and put the box away. "Executive Director," she mused with a small smile. Kind of a grand title for a small nonprofit, but she had to admit that she liked the sound of it. The best part was that, despite the lofty title, she could—and would—get her hands dirty. She would have insisted on that if her new boss hadn't already made clear that she was expected to get involved in each project.

She was back to her roots, back in her adopted home state, and, she blew out a breath, it was about time she got back to work.

As if the very thought was a trigger, Sara's phone rang.

* * *

"Once again, Sara, welcome to the team." Jim Callahan stretched out a long arm and firmly shook her hand as the others rose and left the room. He nodded toward the woman on Sara's left. "I trust Nandini has shown you where everything is?"

Sara nodded, exchanging grins with the other woman. She had sensed immediately a kindred spirit in Nandini, a slightly built woman whose family was still back in Jaipur, India. When she and Sara had been introduced, Sara had immediately nailed Nandini's accent and offered her a greeting in Hindi. Nandini had responded with a rush of dialogue that left Sara laughing and shaking her head, protesting that her knowledge of Hindi was rudimentary, at best. Nandini did speak Nepali, however, and the two women had quickly connected.

She smiled back at Jim. "Absolutely. She's amazing."

With a brief nod, Jim rose and headed toward the door. "When you're finished with HR, I would like to meet with you to go over a new project. I was handling things here while we were conducting the search for a new ED, but it really needs a local's touch." Jim shrugged. "I think I'm a bit too much of an outsider for some of the folks out here, Seattlites are a breed apart." He offered an apologetic smile as he checked his watch. "I'll have just enough time to brief you before I head back to New York." Jim paused, then added, "I'm not sure who's happier you're with us, Sara, me on behalf of CoGS or my family, since I won't need to fly out here every other month." As CEO of

Grassroots Gardens, CoGS' New York-based parent company, Jim had been burning the candle at literally both ends of the country in order to keep things running smoothly until their coalition replaced the executive director in Seattle.

He offered her a larger smile, his long, gaunt face stretching as he did so. He was tall, slim, and graying and resembled a professor she had had in college. Lanky build, hair a bit over his collar, always slightly rumpled. He simply exuded calm, and that was one of the things that had appealed to Sara during her multiple interviews.

"She's nearly finished with her paperwork. I'll send her over as soon as the rest of it is signed." Nandini nodded as Jim held the tall glass door for them, then led Sara back down the hallway to her own office. "Did your mum and dad get settled okay?" She waved Sara into a chair.

"Oh, god. Don't remind me." Sara rubbed her eyes before peeking out between her fingertips. "I think every muscle in my body is aching."

Nandini smiled as she sat down and pulled out a large, blue folder. "I told you that Amandeep and I would be happy to help you. Ajay was with the boys, but we would have been happy to assist."

Smiling, Sara took the forms handed to her and began signing the stack. "I know, and I appreciate it. It's just…" She paused, then shrugged as she looked up. "I really hate to start off a friendship by asking you to lug boxes. I would like to have you all over, though, for dinner soon. I'm getting the house back in order, now." She gave a dramatic shudder. "Boxes. If I never see another one again…" She grinned as Nandini laughed, signed her name one last time, and handed it across the desk.

"So," Nandini neatly stacked the signed paperwork, "I assume you can find the conference room again? When Jim's in town, that's his go-to office space." When Sara nodded, Nandini leaned forward and said quietly, "I don't think I'm giving away any secrets when I say that Jim was quite chuffed that he managed to lure you away from HGI."

Surprised and flattered, Sara looked down for a moment, recalling her reason for leaving her old company and assignment so abruptly, then back up to her new friend. "It was just good timing, I guess. I needed to be...to be home, and you had an opening."

"So. It's all worked out then, in the end?" Nandini gave her a thumbs-up. "I have a feeling you are where you need to be, Sarasvati." She rose and held out a hand. "Welcome, again."

Rising to her feet, Sara nodded and returned the handshake, glad to have made one good friend in her new place, then she headed to find out what it was they had in mind for her first major project. She hoped it was a good one.

CHAPTER THREE

This could not be happening.

Margaret had managed to get through the PowerPoint presentation to the Planning Commission. Her bird-dogging Jeremy to make sure everything was in place had been rewarded with a flawless set of slides and a smooth talk. Only the chair of the commission had any questions, and that didn't really count. James Thompson asked questions whether he had any or not. Margaret hadn't yet determined whether he just liked to hear himself talk or whether he thought his name should always be reflected in the minutes. Either way, she was grateful that no one had anything serious to say about the University District project, because most of her mind was occupied with only one thought.

This could *not* be happening!

As she made her way back upstairs to her office, Margaret wished she hadn't checked her email over lunch at her desk. It was a foolish thought. She had known The Ave's Merchant Association would be sending her an email before the Planning

Commission meeting, and sure enough, there had been a message from Beverly Morgan.

But it was the email from Harold Dieter, the attorney for the Stockton Family Trust that had surprised her. Her finger hovered a moment over the mouse, almost afraid to click the message open. Could this be it? Maybe, at last, the board of trustees had decided to accept the city's bid for the Stockton Industries building. She could see the Pacific Rim Robotics sign in her mind's eye on the new complex, blue and white, adding to the skyline.

Margaret drew a deep breath and clicked the email open.

She had to read it twice before the information penetrated the fog of her dismay.

The board of trustees for the Stockton Family Trust had another offer for the property.

If she couldn't wrap up the Stockton Industries building, the deal with Pacific Rim was dead. How could this have happened? Had some competitor found out about the city's interest and decided to try a bidding war? Or had the board somehow solicited another bidder to drive the price up?

She pushed her niçoise salad away, too queasy to even think of eating. Whatever had happened, she had to fix it. The Mayor's Office wouldn't give her an unlimited amount of money, and if the bidding soared above market value…she shuddered. All that time and money and effort wasted. The beautiful Pacific Rim Robotics building would never be more than lines on the piece of paper in the file room.

The sight of seared tuna lying innocently across the bed of lettuce made her angry, and she dumped the plastic bowl holding it into the wastebasket. The hell with recycling.

She gathered up her file and the printouts for the Planning Commission meeting and tried to think. There had to be something she could do. Something.

It just couldn't be happening.

* * *

By the time she got back from the meeting, Margaret realized she needed more information. There was no way to devise a strategy going forward without tactical intelligence. The question remained: how best to gather the data she needed?

"How did it go?"

"What?" Margaret looked around in surprise.

Jeremy said, "The meeting, Ms. Winter. The Planning Commission. How did it go?"

She'd been passing by his desk, her steps automatic, her mind whirling with possibilities. She looked down at him and blinked. "Oh, fine," she said absently, her mind still busy with battle plans.

"Good," he said. "Glad that PowerPoint presentation was all right."

"Um. Yes. It was fine."

"Did they have any questions?" he continued.

Margaret narrowed her eyes. One inquiry too many. "As always, Chairman Thompson added some useful insights." Her tone was acerbic, but she wasn't going to be caught dead complaining about Thompson to one of her staff. She wouldn't put it past Jeremy to rat her out. "I need for you to do something for me right away."

"Of course." He grabbed his phone and flipped open the cover, tapping the screen a few times before looking up at her expectantly.

"Get me a list of the members of the board of trustees of the Stockton Family Trust. Phone numbers, email addresses, any background information you can get quickly. I want whatever you can get by the end of the day."

His stubby thumbs flew over the virtual keyboard. "Okay. Anything else?"

She almost laughed. As if he would be able to get anything else done in the next two or three hours. "That's all for today," she said over her shoulder. First order of business, she decided, was to call Harold Dieter.

Margaret successfully maneuvered her way through the receptionist, Dieter's secretary, and his legal assistant, all of whom wanted to know exactly what Margaret might be calling about. She used her best "I'm from the government and I'm here to help" tone and finally managed to get an audience with Dieter himself.

"Ms. Winter, how can I help you?" The attorney sounded hurried.

"Thank you so much for taking my call," Margaret said smoothly. "I know you're extremely busy."

As she had hoped, acknowledging his importance calmed him a bit.

"Well, I always have time for a city official. I presume you're calling about my email of this morning."

"Yes," Margaret admitted. "I was certainly…surprised."

"I thought it only fair that we should notify you of the change of situation," he said. "The board hasn't met yet, of course."

"Um…when would that be, can you tell me?"

"The next meeting is set for the twenty-first. I can't promise you that the final decision will be made at that time, of course. The board might want to request further information, perhaps. And they are certainly not obligated to take either offer."

Lawyer talk. Margaret sighed. But it told her something important—"either offer" seemed to limit the potential buyers to two. At least she only had one competitor out there.

"Well, obviously, the city is still very interested in pursuing our bid for the property. I don't suppose you could tell me what the other bid might be." She crossed her fingers.

A rumble came over the phone. Margaret couldn't tell if it was a chuckle or Dieter clearing his throat.

"Well, no. As we would not disclose the amount of the city's bid, of course. But I can tell you the identity of the other bidder. That's not confidential."

Yes, that would help, Margaret calculated swiftly. Whoever it was must need something from the local government. Maybe she could make a deal with…whoever.

"It's from a nonprofit," Dieter continued. "The group's name is Community Gardens of Seattle. CoGS, they're called."

A *garden?* Some do-gooders wanted to turn her wonderful, job-creating, tax-paying industrial headquarters into a garden?

She wrote down the name of the group and made nice noises to Dieter before hanging up. She was not going to lose the Pacific Robotics project to cucumbers and tomatoes.

This really could *not* be happening.

* * *

"This is Sara Chandler."

Margaret was unprepared for the head of CoGS to just pick up her own phone.

"Ah, yes. I…um, I'm Margaret Winters, director of Neighborhood Development for the city." *Drat, stop stuttering. Deep breath. She sounds young and probably inexperienced.*

"How can I help you?"

Margaret had given her approach a bit of thought. Community Gardens had to be run by altruistic and noble people who were under the misguided impression that they knew what was best for everyone. The key here was to convince them that Margaret's plan was really the best solution. Logic always worked.

"Ms. Chandler, I understand that CoGS have a bid pending for a Stockton Industries property on Pine Street."

There was a small pause. "Yes," she heard after a moment.

Well, that was helpful. "You may or may not be aware that the city has made a prior offer for the same property."

"I did not know that, no."

This was like making snowballs in August.

"I would like to talk to you about this situation. You see, the city has a tremendous opportunity to secure a major industry employer if we can acquire this property. It will bring hundreds of jobs to the city, millions of dollars in both direct and indirect benefits to…"

"Ms. Winter, do you know what a food desert is?"

What? Is she even listening? Or just fond of non sequiturs?

"Um, no, what…"

"A food desert is an urban area where it's virtually impossible to buy healthy, affordable, or fresh food. People without their own transportation, without enough money to travel far enough to access the food they need end up subsisting on convenience store or gas station junk."

"Okay." *Where might this be going?*

"There are a lot of ways to address this problem. One of the best is to create community gardens where people can work to grow their own healthy produce right where they live. Growing plants are great for an urban environment, people can get healthier diets, feel a sense of pride and productivity."

How had she managed to take over this argument? "Ms. Chandler, you can hardly compare a garden that could benefit a handful of people with the millions of…"

"It's not always a matter of numbers."

Well, that was heresy of the gravest kind. It was always about the numbers.

Margaret drew in a deep breath, but before she could resume her attack, there was a commotion at the other end of the telephone.

"What?" she heard Sara say to someone else, then she heard, "I'm sorry, Ms. Winters, I have to go. Irrigation pipe crises."

The call clicked off before Margaret could say a word.

She hung up on me? She hung up on me!

* * *

For the first time she could remember, Margaret reached her office door the next morning to find Jeremy hovering nearby. And he wasn't alone. Diana/Dolly/Intern Girl was co-hovering. Margaret was mesmerized for a moment by the tornado of curls on the top of her head.

"Ms. Winter," he greeted her politely. "Sorry to ambush you so early, but we have news."

He was almost quivering with suppressed excitement. He looked more like Emmet the billy goat than ever.

"Well, you had better come in."

He perched on the edge of her visitor's chair, even forgetting to sit on his jacket. Diana/Dolly/Intern Girl kept fidgeting with her hands. Together they were making Margaret nervous. She waved a hand at Jeremy to get him talking.

"We were doing the research about Stockton Industries and the family trust and we—well, really, Daisy—found out about a connection to CoGS. I knew you would want to know right away."

Daisy blushed as if Jeremy had accused her of some salacious act.

"And that would be?"

"Tell her, Daisy," Jeremy said.

Margaret was not entirely happy with this turn of events. She didn't mind Jeremy having an intern, not really, but she didn't expect to be required to actually interact with her. Now she was going to have to remember her name. Daisy. Think flowers. Margaret sighed. *Honestly, who named their kid Daisy and expected her to be taken seriously?* She narrowed her eyes and refocused on the nervous young woman.

Daisy pushed up her oversized glasses with an index finger.

"The Stockton Family trust was established in 1951 by Jeremiah Stockton and his wife Blanche after they made a fortune in the paper and lumber industry. It has continued to be successful in its investment strategy, accumulating various real estate holdings throughout the…"

Margaret lifted a hand. "Stop. I mean this sincerely. I. Don't. Care. Particularly about what happened seventy years ago. What on earth does this have to do with the situation with the Stockton Industries building?"

Jeremy said, "Just cut to the chase, Daisy."

Something in his tone seemed a bit familiar. Margaret eyed him. Might he be having an affair with Intern Girl Daisy? More and more like Emmet the goat.

Daisy fiddled with her glasses again. Did she ever sit still?

"Jeremiah's daughter married a man named Chandler," she said. "Sara Chandler is a Stockton and a beneficiary of the family trust."

Margaret actually understood for the first time the true meaning of thunderstruck.

"You're not serious," she said at last.

"I double checked it," Daisy said. "The Chandlers don't really use the money. They donate almost all of it to various causes, and Sara seems to do the same. But she's a Stockton on her mother's side, definitely."

This was a disaster. What chance did she have against a family connection? The Pacific Rim building was vanishing in her mind's eye in wisps of blue and white smoke.

Stop. Think. If this were already a done deal, wouldn't Harold Dieter have pretty much said so?

Why would they bid, then? she asked herself.

She realized she had spoken aloud when Jeremy cleared his throat meaningfully.

"Spit it out," Margaret said tartly.

"We can't really confirm it, but it seems the CoGS offer was a combination of some cash, though certainly nowhere near fair market value. The benefit would be a huge amount of charitable deduction. So, this might just come down to the tax liability situation for the trust, nothing to do with the money per se."

Nothing to do with the money. Margaret could hardly wrap her mind around the concept.

There was only one way out of this that she could see. If she concealed what she knew about Sara Chandler, maybe she could still use the logic of the situation to talk CoGS out of demanding this site.

"Jeremy, I want you to find another place for CoGS," she said suddenly.

"What?"

"Another site for the garden. Any place else but the Stockton Industries building. City-owned or not, any property we think we can acquire. The more options the better. And ASAP, understand? The clock is ticking."

The harder part, of course, would be persuading CoGS to choose another site. Margaret was sure she would have to persuade the director that it was the best solution for everyone.

She had never doubted her ability to persuade anyone to do almost anything. Well, she hadn't been able to talk her mother out of the goat cheese-making business, but other than that…

This had to work.

CHAPTER FOUR

Sara dug her fingers into the dirt, absently noting the moisture and texture as she deftly transferred seedlings from their starter pots to the fertile ground of the garden. Her movements were smooth, automatic, years of practice making the simple task something she could do while her mind worked on other things. With the last of the little green plants in place, she sat back on her heels and, after brushing the worst of the crumbling soil off, let her hands fall to rest on her knees, still planted in the dirt.

Tipping her head back, Sara closed her eyes and enjoyed the warmth of the too-often-missing Seattle sun bathing her face. A slight breeze brought with it the familiar scents of coming rain mixed with sea, freshly turned soil, and sun-warmed and thriving plants.

"So, is this what you're calling 'work' these days?"

Dropping her chin, Sara lifted a hand and shoved the brim of her well-worn boonie hat upward. "Huh. Look at what the cat dragged in." She grinned at the newcomer and began to rise, only to settle back again as the woman waved her off.

"There had better *not* be a cat around here!"

"Pretty sure you're safe, Kel." Despite her visitor's indication that she need not get up, Sara stood and wrapped her arms around her ex-girlfriend. For a fleeting moment she let herself remember with pleasure the strength and warmth she had enjoyed in those arms. Kelly's familiar chest-to-pelvis full-body hug...*ooh*. "Not only do I clearly remember your aversion to any animal, I doubt you would find one this high up."

Kelly looked around the rooftop garden and nodded. "Pretty cool, Sara. Looks like things are working out well with Home Grown, then."

"It did. It was, I mean. As you may have figured out as you made your way up here, I've moved over to Community Gardens of Seattle. I love their model and programs." Sara led the way over to a small wooden table set back under a makeshift awning. Pulling out two worn water bottles, she handed one to Kelly. Downing nearly half of her own, Sara took a deep breath, realizing she was hotter than she had realized. "Glad you stopped by. Guess I needed a break."

"Glad I could help." She looked Sara up and down, her eyebrows raised. "I don't really remember you as a 'Daisy Duke' kind of girl."

Sara looked down at her cut-off denim shorts, complete with worn, ragged white threads hanging down in a quasi-fringe ringing both thighs. She grimaced. "Mom's. I, ah, need to do laundry."

"Oh, my God! You're *still* stealing clothes! I can't believe you stole shorts from Sandy!"

Sara shot Kelly a mock frown and both women started laughing. Sara's penchant for raiding wardrobes had driven Kelly crazy during their relationship. One thing in a long list.

After a few moments, they settled down and Kelly handed Sara back her still-full bottle. "Here, I don't really need it." She waited until Sara replaced the bottle in the cooler. "I, ah, called your mom, trying to find you."

Sara winced. "Ooh. Sorry."

"Yeah." She shrugged. "It is what it is. Anyway..." Kelly walked to the edge of the fenced rooftop and looked over.

"Wild, a garden up here, a city down there." She turned and leaned back against the waist-high concrete wall. "How've you been, Sara?"

Tilting her head, Sara lifted a shoulder. "Good. Pretty good, anyway." She took another sip of her water, pushing aside thoughts of Devery, of the last few months. Pushing aside the guilt.

"So, your mom told me you've been in Tibet. Getting back to your roots?" Kelly's quirky smile was gentle.

"Something close to that, I guess. It was the nearest posting. We, er...*I* was doing an intensive online course in French while I was there and planning on heading to Madagascar at the end of the year." Quashing the wave of guilt that again bubbled up, she frowned and studied her bottle of water.

Kelly stepped away from the wall and moved closer. "Sandy told me about your girlfriend. I'm sorry."

Blinking back the sudden sting of tears, Sara shrugged and took a long drink of her water. She didn't want to talk about this and especially not with Kelly. Once upon a time she had thought it was Kelly she would tell everything to. Share everything with. They had made plans, talked about a future, wandered various old Seattle neighborhoods and talked about reclaiming some of the old homes there. Then they had graduated and, just like that, it was over. Kelly suddenly had plans that didn't include her and Sara was expected to go along with them. It had taken a long time for Sara to get to a place where they could again be friends. Friends, yes, but not close enough that she wanted to talk about Devery. About her own cowardice. About how she had taken the first chance Devery had offered and run.

Disgusted with herself all over again, Sara once again shoved all that down and closed the lid. "So," she said, setting aside her water bottle and drying her hands on the edge of her tee. "I'm sure you didn't hunt me down just to say hi. What's up?"

Kelly's face tensed up and she shoved her hands into her pockets, her shoulders hunching as she spoke, her early casual posture now rigid. "I wanted to, um...well, the thing is—"

"Jesus, Kel. What's got you wound up?" Sara frowned at her ex, the most straightforward and, well,...*blunt* person she knew. She looked like a toddler caught stealing cookies. If Kelly had something to say, she usually just said it and dealt with the aftermath. "Spit it out."

"I'mgettingmarried."

Sara blinked. Whatever she had said, it had come out as one giant word. "Sorry? Was that English?"

Kelly took a deep breath, turned, then lifted her head to look Sara squarely in the eye. "I am getting married."

"You...oh." The air left her lungs in a whoosh and she dropped into the chair behind her. Kelly "I Don't Do Commitment" Saunders was getting married.

Well. Well then. Good for her. Fucking good for her. Zippity doo dah. Throw a parade. Wa-hooo. A myriad of other less-than-positive comments ran through Sara's brain, but chief among them were Kelly's last words to her as she left that final time. *"It's not you, Sara, it's me. I'm just not made that way." Yada, yada.*

"So, I guess you are made that way, after all."

"Sara..."

Sara looked up at Kelly. "'Sara,' *what*? Congratulations," she added with a dry smile.

Kelly stepped forward and dropped to her knees beside Sara's chair. "Sara...I wanted...I really wanted to be the one to tell you, so you didn't hear it from someone else." She rested her forearms on the arm of the old wooden chair. "I know we didn't end things in the most—"

"'*We*' didn't end things, Kel. *You* ended it. Ended us."

"I did. And I know I did it badly, and I'm so, so sorry."

Taking a deep breath, Sara slowly shook her head. "No...it's...I'm fine. It was a long time ago and I'm over it. Honestly, I really am," she added, reaching out to squeeze Kelly's arm. "It's just...you caught me at a weird time and I *really* wasn't expecting to ever hear you say those words."

She patted Kelly's arm again and stood up. "It *was* a long time ago, Kel. You moved on and so did I. I really *am* okay. And," Sara paused, cocking her head to one side, "I wish you the best. I really do."

"Thank you." Kelly rose to her feet, brushing dirt from her shorts. "I appreciate that." She stepped forward and reached for Sara, giving her a light kiss before wrapping her in another hug.

Sara closed her eyes and let herself enjoy, one last time, the slightly spicy scent of Kelly's cologne, the warmth of being held closely by someone who knew you, inside and out. She had missed this, just being held. In the last few months of their time together Devery simply *couldn't* hold her and wouldn't allow Sara to do the holding. She hadn't realized how much she had missed that simple contact until now. They held one another for a long moment in the late afternoon sunlight, Sara tucked against Kelly's chest, her head resting just below her ex's chin. She had just started to step back when a rich, velvety voice interrupted her thoughts.

* * *

Margaret stopped abruptly. Sara wasn't alone. Or, rather, there were two women in the rooftop garden, and she wasn't sure which was the woman she was looking for. Neither fit the voice on the phone to her mind, unless cargo shorts and a T-shirt were de rigueur for CEOs of nonprofits these days. Or frayed denim shorts and a tee that stretched over solid shoulders and hugged biceps. It was a coin toss, really. Denim Cutoffs was looking up at a woman standing near her, a little too close for casual conversation. Margaret eyed both more carefully. The other woman had close-cropped dark hair and was wearing, yes, Birkenstocks. If Denim Cutoffs had pinged Margaret's gaydar, old Cargo Shorts pinned her gaydar firmly at DEFCON 1.

Cargo Shorts said something Margaret couldn't hear, and Denim Cutoffs smiled. Margaret fumed, determinedly *not* tapping a foot in impatience. *Oh, don't mind me, I have all day to stand and watch you two…commune. I just have some business to discuss.* "Excuse me."

The women pulled apart, and Denim Cutoffs turned to face her.

Margaret's gaze flickered between Denim Cutoffs and Cargo Shorts, then her eyes tightened slightly. "Sorry to… interrupt," she said, knowing she did not sound at all sorry. "I'm Margaret Winters."

"Oh." Denim glanced over and saw Margaret waiting. She stepped forward and gave Cargo a hug, carefully keeping her dirt-covered fingers away from her shorts and her T-shirt. *I mean really*, Margaret thought, *who irons their T-shirts*?

Cargo Shorts returned the hug and followed up with a light kiss. On the mouth.

Well, that settled that. Margaret instantly analyzed the kiss. Too long for "just friends," too short for "I'll see you tonight at home for a lot more than a kiss." Just right for "We used to be lovers but aren't anymore, but we're still friends."

It also settled the question of which one of the women was her quarry. Cargo Shorts came down the graveled path toward Margaret, her Birkenstocks making little crunchy sounds. She had an attractive face and was clearly partly of Korean or Chinese descent. She gave Margaret a careful look, half-appraising and half-appreciative. If Margaret hadn't already been fuming, she would have preened a bit. As it was, she delivered her best frosty look and proceeded down the path toward Sara. It took most of her concentration not to catch a heel in the gravel.

"Hi," Sara said. "Margaret. We meet at last."

She was smiling. She had a nice smile and Margaret found that annoying. She was also annoyed by the assumption that they were on a first-name basis.

"Ms. Chandler," she said coolly. "I tried reaching you several times, but you don't answer your phone, apparently."

"I'm spending most of this week on sites, and I don't have a cell."

"You don't ha—" She shook her head in disbelief. "Who, in 2020, doesn't have a cell phone?"

Sara shrugged, clearly unconcerned. "Me, obviously."

Margaret watched her, still irritated. Honestly, those cut-offs were too short for any woman over the age of twelve. Sara wasn't very tall, but she had sturdy, shapely legs with well-defined muscles, far from model-thin.

Margaret looked up to see Sara still smiling, this time in amusement. *Crap, she probably thinks I was checking out her legs!*

"Until recently I lived in places with minimal cell service."

The concept of an adult, especially a businesswoman, not owning, let alone relying on, a cell phone baffled Margaret and her expression must have reflected it. Sara continued, "I never felt the need. I like focusing on the quiet, on what the sun and the wind and the soil is saying to me. Phone calls can be irritating."

She thinks dirt talks to her. She's worse than my mother.

"Anyway, you must have really wanted to chat if you came all the way down here," Sara said. "Come over and sit down a minute."

Margaret expected they would go inside the neighborhood association building next door, but Sara led her to a bench tucked under a tree. Margaret didn't know what kind of tree it was, but she figured Sara probably knew its name. Maybe in Latin, or maybe she called it George or something.

Sara reached down to a small cooler and plucked out a large plastic container and a paper cup. "Can I offer you some fruit water? I make it myself."

Of course she did.

Margaret shook her head. The bottle had an infuser inserted into the center that was filled with blueberries and strawberries and something orange-ish. Mango? Sara poured out a healthy libation and drank it down thirstily.

Of course she wouldn't use bottled water, Margaret thought. It's probably triple-filtered water imported from Tahiti or Bangkok or somewhere. Organic fruit, of course.

"So what's on your mind, Margaret?" Sara asked cheerfully.

"Did you get your irrigation pipe crises solved?" Margaret didn't care, but she hoped this conversational gambit would prompt the apology she was owed. No such luck.

"We did," Sara said. "Just a loose joint. Thanks for asking."

So annoying.

"We didn't finish our discussion yesterday," Margaret began again.

"Really? I thought we were both really clear."

"That's not the same as finishing our negotiation," Margaret pointed out.

Sara tipped her head back against the bark and seemed to be studying George's leaves waving in the breeze. "Is that what you thought we were doing? Negotiating?"

"What else?"

"Maybe just stating our positions."

Margaret felt confused. "What's the point of stating a position," she said, "if it's not preliminary to negotiating?"

Sara tipped her head down to meet Margaret's gaze. "Just to be clear," she said. "Then we know where we are and there aren't any misunderstandings."

"It's not about misunderstandings," Margaret said. "We have to resolve this."

Sara said thoughtfully, "Well, no. We really don't."

"I...uh...what?"

"We don't have to resolve it," Sara repeated patiently.

Did the woman not understand English? "Of course we do. We have to decide what's happening to the property."

"That's not our decision to make, Margaret," Sara said quietly.

"Of course it is. Look, this project means a lot to the city, to the taxpayers, and all the future jobs that will be created by..."

"You told me all this yesterday," Sara interrupted. "I understand. This site means a lot to the people *in* this city." She deliberately used Margaret's phrasing to make her point.

"We can find another place..." Margaret began.

"I don't want to have yesterday's argument over again. I'm not going to convince you. You're not going to convince me. Let's not fight about it."

"We're not..." Margaret drew a deep breath. "Look, if we don't discuss it, how are we going to decide what to do?"

"We're not," Sara repeated. "The board will donate it to the association. Or sell it to the city. Or do something else entirely. It's not up to us."

Margaret stared at her. The concept that she couldn't influence, or even determine, the outcome of the situation was so foreign to her that she actually had trouble grasping the idea.

"But we can talk to them, tell them what would be the best course of action, show them the impact of..." Margaret knew she was babbling.

Sara touched her arm to stop her. Margaret looked down. Sara's fingertips were warm, like sunshine on her skin.

"The board will consider everything and make whatever they think is the best decision."

Margaret stood up abruptly.

"You're just saying that because you know they'll do what you want!" she exclaimed. "You're a member of the family! This whole bid is probably just a formality!"

So much for her strategy of keeping information to herself. There was just something about Sara Chandler that made her a little crazy.

"It is certainly a genuine bid. CoGS is a separate entity from me. We picked the best site and made a fair offer. You're really off base here!" Sara snapped. Margaret felt an odd satisfaction at having finally gotten a reaction from her.

"The board isn't just responsible to me, you know," Sara continued. "They have to do the best thing for the whole family who are beneficiaries of the trust. Just because I want the property doesn't mean they'll donate it to us."

"Look," Margaret said. Maybe if she kept repeating the facts, Granola Girl would eventually catch on. "This project will mean hundreds of jobs for people in this area. Huge economic gains. Tax cuts for the city. A long-term relationship with Pacific Rim will benefit thousands of citizens. Wake up, Miss Chandler, this is *reality*."

"And this garden means food for families who will never qualify for those benefits!" Shaking her head, Sara picked up a rag and began to scrub the dirt off her hands. "I don't know what reality you live in, but your reality is far different from mine."

Margaret didn't believe any of it. But she wasn't going to stand here and beat her head against...a tree trunk. "This isn't over," she said to Sara. "Not even close."

She stalked away down the gravel path, her exit somewhat marred by nearly tripping over one of the small stones lining the walkway.

Damn Sara Chandler anyway.

* * *

After a quick shower and a fast dinner, Margaret propped herself up in bed with her secret pleasure: a romance novel. This was her favorite time, the workday behind her and a nice Saturday morning sleep-in to look forward to. She could read as late as she wanted. She was in the midst of a luxurious stretch when she remembered: she hadn't called her mother back... again. Second time this month.

Drat. If I don't call her, she'll think I've been mugged or raped or fallen in the bathtub and call the National Guard. Suck it up, buttercup.

No way around it. She sighed and picked up her phone.

"Dusty! I was starting to worry about you."

"I'm fine, Mother."

"I worry about you in the big city, you know."

"Seattle is a very safe place, you know.

"Oh, my dear. There are no safe places anymore."

Well, that wasn't a topic she wanted to explore. In Margaret's world, safety was your personal responsibility, and she took charge of her own life. Her mother had drifted from place to place, dragging her child with her. Whether it was staying with friends, long before "couch surfing" became a thing, settling in a *kibbutz*, living and working in a commune, her childhood had been one relocation after another.

Her grandparents had tried to step in, but as long as "Dusty" was receiving an education and was not being abused, they had no grounds to try to take her away. Mind you, having met her grandparents, there was a part of Margaret that was secretly glad about that. She wasn't sure which would have been worse: growing up as a tumbleweed, bouncing from pillar to post, or growing up essentially in a starched cage, rarely seeing her grandparents and being raised by a succession of maids and/or nannies. She shuddered. Time for a change of subject. There was at least one reliable choice.

Margaret asked, "How are the girls?"

"Oh!" It always pleased her mother when Margaret asked about them. "Fine. I was afraid Maybelline had scrapie, but it turns out she had just bumped against a rough patch of the fence. We're putting some balm on it."

"The fence?"

"No, dear, on Maybelline. She's feeling better already."

"You made the balm yourself, I'm sure," Margaret said dryly.

"Of course. Natural remedies are the best, you know. And great news: Annabelle is pregnant."

"Well, that's nice."

"It is! She's a great mother. And I think it might be twins this time. Isn't that exciting?"

"Wonderful."

"You know that offer to come home and work with me here is always open."

"I appreciate it, Mother, but I'm really not the farm girl type."

"I don't know why not. You grew up in the country."

Well, that's one way of putting it. Communes and kibbutzim and co-ops. Weird food and never enough hot water.

"I like where I live, Mother. I'm fond of indoor plumbing."

Her mother produced a delicate snort. "You're never going to let that one go, are you? It was one place, and there was plumbing. It simply didn't always work."

Margaret felt a tiny niggle of guilt as her mother blew out a long sigh. Before she could say anything, her mother spoke again. "And how was work today, Dusty?"

"Mother, stop calling me that. Work is good. It's excellent, in fact. Things are going very well."

"Well, that's nice. So, what you need is someone to share it with."

And here we go. So much for hoping she'd forgotten this morning's topic.

"I appreciate your concern, Mother, I do. But I don't like blind dates."

"You need to be open to what the Universe sends you. Clearly these people were put in my path so that our daughters could meet. She could be the one, Dusty."

Margaret rolled her eyes dramatically.

"There is no such thing as 'The One.'" She slid the romance novel under the spare pillow so it wouldn't hear her heretical sentiments. She wouldn't want the characters to go off their predetermined path to Happily Ever After. "Relationships take hard work and time and right now I'm focused on my career."

"Things happen when they are meant to happen," her mother said serenely. "You just need to be ready for the experience. From everything Sandy, her mother, says, Sarasvati is a wonderful young woman."

That's what everyone's mother thinks. Margaret scrubbed a hand across her brow and shook her head. She was not going to win this argument. It would cost less time and energy if she just agreed to the date. She could waste two hours on a date with some woman she would never see again, or she could spend the next two weeks arguing with her mother about it. And arguing with her mother was like trying to punch water. She just kept flowing right back at her.

"Okay, okay," Margaret muttered. "Blind date it is."

"Oh, my dear, you won't be sorry, I'm sure."

I'm already sorry, Margaret thought.

CHAPTER FIVE

What do you wear, Margaret wondered, *when you* don't *want to make a good impression?*

She wasn't used to thinking like this. She stood in her closet and contemplated her options, tapping one forefinger against her chin. Her work clothes were carefully coordinated and accessorized to enhance her position as a power player. Her athletic wardrobe was designed for function and a flattering fit—just in case the woman from the eighth floor happened to be on the stair climber wearing those black running tights.

Everything else was pretty much old sweaters and T-shirts, not exactly suitable for a blind date. Even a date where she was sure she would never want to see the woman again.

A knock on her front door saved her from further consternation.

"Hello, dear," Mrs. Stein said when Margaret opened her door. "I know I'm a little early. I'm not interrupting you, am I?"

"No, not at all," Margaret said. "I lost track of the time. Come on in."

Mrs. Stein, she reflected, probably had no trouble deciding what to wear for any occasion. Margaret had never seen her neighbor in anything other than a cardigan and matching short-sleeved pullover—which Mrs. Stein called a "twin set"—and a skirt. Today it was the blue plaid skirt, with the solid blue sweaters picking up the color from the pattern perfectly. Margaret had to give Mrs. Stein credit: she always matched her colors.

What Margaret could not understand was why a woman well into her seventies would voluntarily get dressed every morning in a skirt, hose, and heels. Surely she had earned the right to wear, say, yoga pants once in a while.

With a little pang, she remembered that Mrs. Stein had nowhere she needed to be most days, no one to talk to. Maybe she was afraid that if she didn't get dressed up, she might spend all day in her bathrobe.

"New hair stylist?" Margaret asked as she got Mrs. Stein settled at the tiny kitchen table.

"Same hair dresser, new style." Mrs. Stein patted her fluffy gray hair with fingers tangled with age. "What do you think? Marion said she thought I could use a shorter cut to give it some lift."

"Looks great," Margaret said. "And you got a manicure, too."

Mrs. Stein smiled. "Nothing makes a girl feel nicer than pink nail polish."

"That is a universal truth," Margaret agreed. "What'll it be today? I have Irish breakfast, some of that peach tea, or the white jasmine you like."

Mrs. Stein gave this question grave consideration, the lines on her face settling in a familiar pattern, a lifetime of thinking about what to have for teatime. Margaret wondered how her skin could look so weathered while her eyes remained bright and youthful.

"That depends," she finally said. "Are we having the shortbread, the spice cake, or the lemon bars?"

Margaret laughed at her question.

"You know me so well."

"Oh, my dear, we've been having Saturday afternoon tea almost every week for two years. I know all your bakery weaknesses by now."

"You do," Margaret admitted. "I got the lemon bars today."

"Then the Irish breakfast. We don't want the fruit flavors fighting and the jasmine is too delicate for the lemon. It's better with the shortbread cookies."

"Irish breakfast tea it is," Margaret said cheerfully. She put her kettle on and scooped out the tea.

They got comfortable at the table as the tea was steeping. The lemon bars with their snowy skiff of powdered sugar were arranged on the plate between them.

"You really do look especially nice today," Margaret said. "Did you have a good week?"

Mrs. Stein added a splash of cream to the bottom of her teacup.

"Well, Leonard called me yesterday. He and the family are coming to see me next month, when Benny gets out of school. That will be fun."

"That's great! What will you do while they're here?"

Mrs. Stein checked on her tea. Not ready yet. She managed a disingenuous smile.

"Packing, I imagine," she said coyly.

"Wh-what? You mean, like for a trip?"

Mrs. Stein was beaming at her now. Margaret felt her heart stutter.

"No, my dear. That's my big news. I'm moving to San Diego! Leonard worries about me, you know, and he said he wanted me close. So—you won't believe it!—he found a one-bedroom unit right in his own building. I'm going to live one floor above them!"

Margaret poured her tea, too stunned to speak. Mrs. Stein was moving?

"My dear, you look upset. I thought you would be happy for me."

"I—I am, of course. It's wonderful. You'll be able to see your grandson all the time, and Leonard won't worry so much about you…but what about all your friends here? We'll—they'll miss you."

"Dear Margaret." Mrs. Stein patted her hand gently. "I'll miss you so much. But most of the friends George and I had are gone now—retirement homes or off with their families or in the cemetery. Besides, George is always with me wherever I go."

George Stein had been dead for a decade, Margaret knew. She looked fearfully at Mrs. Stein. Had she suddenly become senile? Maybe the whole moving-to-San-Diego story was a figment of her imagination.

Mrs. Stein chuckled, apparently reading her mind.

"I'm fine, dear. I know George is gone. But once you love someone like I loved George, you never really lose them." She twinkled at Margaret, then calmly picked up her teapot and poured out her Irish breakfast tea. "My wish for you is to find someone like that."

Why, oh why, was everyone trying to pair her up?

Mrs. Stein leaned confidentially across the table.

"You're a lovely person, Margaret, but your life is all about working. That's not so good. You're not happy enough. You need something to make you happy."

"I *am* happy," Margaret insisted.

Mrs. Stein plucked a lemon bar from the plate and took a delicate nibble. Several grains of powdered sugar drifted onto the table like the first few snowflakes of an upcoming blizzard.

"My dear. By the time you get to be my age, you've found out a few things. And the most important thing is to know what the most important thing is."

"Um. What?"

Mrs. Stein blew gently onto her tea and took a tentative sip.

"Very good. You do make a nice cup of tea. So many people don't let the tea leaves steep long enough. You don't get the flavor that way."

Margaret took a small gulp of her own tea and burned her tongue. Mrs. Stein often wandered down conversational cul-de-sacs, but this seemed like a longer detour than usual.

"The most important thing?" she prompted Mrs. Stein.

"Oh, yes." Mrs. Stein leaned back comfortably. She rapped a pink-painted fingernail once on the table.

"Everyone needs a reason. To be here, I mean. It can be your cause, or your art, or a child, or anything you love, really. But you have to have love. Something that matters more than anything, something that gives you a purpose. Something you love. Without it, you'll never be happy."

Margaret took a bite of lemon bar, tangy citrus and sweet flaky dough making a satisfying blend of flavors. She said, "I've never heard you say anything like that before."

"Well, we had to have time to become friends, didn't we? But I'm starting a new time in my life now, and I want to leave you with what you need."

"I have my work," Margaret defended herself. "I love my job."

Mrs. Stein pursed her lips. "No, you don't. You like your job. You like being self-supporting. You like being useful. But that's not the same as loving something."

Margaret munched through another bite of lemon bar. Was Mrs. Stein right? And if she was, how would Margaret find something else to do she loved?

A sudden picture came to her of Sara in the garden, digging in the mulch, patting down the soil. The sunshine gleamed on her arms and the light breeze stirred strands of her hair.

I bet she loves her silly plants and playing in the dirt.

She pushed the thought away. "You know what?" Margaret said cheerily. "I could use a fashion consultation. I have a date tonight. How about we go into my walk-in and figure out what I should wear?"

Mrs. Stein beamed at her. Maybe the blind date wouldn't be so bad after all.

* * *

The light afternoon rain had cleared by the time Margaret left for the restaurant. May was usually sunny in Seattle, and sure enough, the sunset looked like it would be beautiful. A few blue-gray clouds hung in the sky over Puget Sound to the west of the city, just enough to catch the setting sun's rays in a couple of hours. As much as Margaret loved a pretty sunset, she appreciated the table where she had been seated, where she could enjoy the view without being blinded. The curving cantilevered balcony was encased in glass, offering a panoramic view of the Seattle port and all of its water traffic. She shrugged the strap of her leather messenger bag/briefcase over her head and tucked in down between her chair and the wall, enjoying the sensation, as she always did, of the supple, worn brown leather as it slid through her fingers.

The harbor was busy, as it always was. Ferries lumbering in and out, small boats zipping around. It was relaxing to sit and watch other people be busy for a change. She glanced at her watch and sighed. How much time would she have to devote to this exercise in futility? That it would be futile she had no doubt. No woman her mother approved of could possibly be remotely interesting to her.

What would this woman—*Sarasvati*, she reminded herself—want to talk about? Perhaps the advantages of essential oils or foot reflexology or guided meditation, whatever the hell that was. Margaret doubted whoever it was would be interested in hearing about her troubles with Stockton Industries. Which was a pity, since that was about the only thing she had been able to think about all week.

She nodded absently to the waiter who delivered the glass of wine she'd asked for as she'd been seated. The water beading on the glass caught the filtered red-gold of the sunset as she sipped the light chardonnay, appreciating its crisp tang. Closing her eyes, she leaned back in her chair and let her mind go where it clearly wanted.

She had spent hours going over the background information on Community Gardens of Seattle. They had a board of directors, but Sara Chandler was clearly the driving force in the sudden increased activism in the organization. Before Sara's arrival on the scene, CoGS had been, well, small potatoes. But recently the Community Gardens of Seattle had scored a major grant from the State of Washington, won a minor award from HUD, and acquired three small sites in the city to set up community gardens. The Stockton Industries site was by far the most ambitious project CoGS had attempted so far. Maybe Margaret could convince Sara that she was in way over her head on the size of the project.

Jeremy's research included some background information on Sara herself, and Margaret had combed through it, trying to figure out who Sara Chandler was and what would work to convince her. Everything she read showed her that Sara was a genuine, bona-fide, twenty-four carat Peace Corps baby. Granola Girl, indeed. Born in Nepal, she had no siblings and had, at least until recently, no permanent residence.

There was no record of her education until college, when she had attended Washington State University for her undergraduate degree after...*Huh, she started at a community college. That's surprising*.

Margaret's eyebrows had raised when she saw the list of publications attached to Sara's name. *Impressive*, she mused, *despite being a Cougar*. Margaret's own University of Washington Husky pride sneered at the clearly lesser, in her mind, Washington State College and its mascot. Curious, she had pulled up the college listed for Sara's graduate degree and studied the majors offered, snorting at what she found. Who knew you could earn a degree in "urban agriculture and gardening education"? And online, no less. *Honestly, an online degree? Please*.

Reading about Sara's college journey had brought back memories of her own. She herself had planned to go the community college route to save money, but in the end had given in to unbending pressure from her grandparents and accepted their help, something her mother had steadfastly refused to do, knowing their assistance always came with strings. Which is why she had negotiated ruthlessly with her parents to ensure that Margaret's subsidized education came with no stipulations.

For all her other odd qualities, her mom was one hell of a negotiator. Maybe she could call her to handle Sara Chandler for her. She and Sara would undoubtedly communicate beautifully.

Of course, before they finished drinking their ethically sourced fair trade coffee her mother would also be organizing an active picketing schedule against Pacific Rim. Margaret shuddered at the thought.

Okay, calm down, she told herself as she sipped her wine again. Just get through an hour or two with this woman, and then you can go back to solving this problem.

Pulling her gaze from the view, she scanned the restaurant, looking for a woman wearing a red hat, the agreed-upon signal. Such a romance novel cliché. At least it wasn't a rose in her lapel. She glanced at her watch and frowned, then scanned the room again. She…spotted the hat. In the next instant, she realized that what had been an awful week could, in fact, become even more horrible.

CHAPTER SIX

Her mother would probably have said that the Universe had conspired to bring Margaret to this cosmic moment in order to gather all her problems together in one place, to get closure or some such nonsense. She watched as Sara Chandler rose from the table where she had been sitting, a jaunty red beret perched on her fluffy hair. She looked as shocked as Margaret felt, but instead of running out the back door, she was actually walking toward her.

This could *not* be happening. How had she missed that red beret when she'd been seated?

"What a surprise," Sara said. "I guess you're here to meet me."

"Well, no. I mean, um…" she trailed off. *No, I'm undercover and I've come to deliver a coded message to the chief. No, I'm a secret restaurant reviewer. No, I'm actually lost.*

Glancing around, almost desperately, for another attractive woman sporting a jaunty red beret, she sighed. "Yes," she admitted, faintly. Clearing her voice, she tried again. "Well, unless another woman, a, uh…" again she paused, not really knowing how to phrase what she was thinking. "I guess I was expecting someone…else," she finished lamely.

Sara nodded her thanks to the waiter who pulled her chair out and held it while she sat, then set her own glass of wine before her. "Let me guess, you were looking for someone who better fit your image of the name 'Sarasvati.'" She smiled into her wineglass as she waited.

"Actually, yes." That was as good a way to put it as any, she thought.

Sara smiled at her, and Margaret felt a little prickling on the back of her neck. What on earth was that about?

"I must have missed you when you came in, sorry." She held up a small device. "I was reading." Sara held out her hand and Margaret took it automatically. "Sarasvati Chandler," she said with an impish smile. "'Sara' to my friends. Nice to meet you."

A bit put out, Margaret returned the handshake perfunctorily. "Look, I'm sorry," she began, keeping her voice cool. "Obviously I had no idea that it would be you, though it seems that wasn't the case with you. It's no problem. I'll just leave." She was irritated. She felt a bit like she'd been played or tricked in some way, and she didn't like it.

Sara held on to Margaret's hand for just a moment. Just as it had when Sara touched her in the garden, Margaret could feel warmth flowing from Sara into her skin. *Stop that!* She pulled her hand free and crossed her arms up to cross them over her chest—and to break the feeling that being in contact with Sara gave her.

"You don't have to do that," Sara said. "We're here. Stay. And," perhaps sensing Margaret's irritation, she continued, "no, I didn't know it was going to be you, per sé. I knew I was meeting a 'Margaret' and that she…you…would be carrying a leather messenger bag and would likely be in a suit." She shrugged apologetically. "Like I said, I was reading, or I would have said something before you were seated."

Margaret looked down at the device Sara was putting back into her bag. "You have a Kindle but you don't carry a cell phone?"

"Hey, these things hold a charge for *weeks* and holds thousands of books." She lifted a shoulder and sipped her wine. "What can I say? I like to read."

Margaret was going to leave, she really was. But she felt herself relax, just the tiniest bit, despite her telling her body to reach for her bag and to stand. Clearly there was something wrong with the connection between her feet and her brain. She should check on that.

She wished Sara looked ridiculous in that red beret—anyone else would—but it sort of fit her. It gave her a slightly bohemian look, along with the light denim shirt she was wearing and the colorful woven vest with geometric patterns in red, yellow, and blue picking up the more subtle colors in her long skirt.

"Nice vest," Margaret said, scrambling for a conversational gambit.

Sara said, "Thank you. It's Peruvian. They make the most amazing clothes. This is alpaca wool. Feel it, isn't it wonderful?"

Margaret took a large gulp of her wine, for some reason her throat suddenly felt dry. She leaned across the table and brushed her hand against the shoulder of the vest, staying far away from the danger zone of a rather nice décolleté visible at the V of the unbuttoned shirt.

Sara's face and chest were tan from her work in the sun, but Margaret could just see the edge of creamy white curves. She pulled her eyes and hand away quickly and said, "Very nice. Have you been to Peru?"

Sara laughed. It sounded like a breeze rippling through autumn leaves.

"I've lived there. And in Nepal and Tibet and several other places you've probably never heard of."

Margaret nodded. "That's a lot of traveling."

"My parents were volunteers with the Peace Corps. They taught school, mostly, all over the world. I grew up everywhere."

A fleeting look of…something…flashed across her face, too fast for Margaret to identify it. She knew a lot of Sara's background already, but it was still interesting to hear her talk about it. And she really didn't want the woman to know she had basically pulled everything short of an FBI file on her. *Know your enemy*, she thought. Sure, that was the reason. It had nothing to do with wanting to know more about the woman who made her own fruity water. Nope, nothing. Margaret took a fortifying sip of her chardonnay, savoring its smooth, buttery finish. She could do this.

"What was that like?" Margaret asked.

"It was…" Sara searched for a word and came up with, "Amazing. Wonderful. Sometimes lonely. But mostly amazing. I learned so much and experienced so many things without even knowing how lucky I was."

Interested despite herself, Margaret took another sip of her wine. They had a lot more in common than Sara probably realized. "I'm guessing you speak some languages."

"A few. My French is pretty good." Again that brief tightening around the eyes, a slight darkening of her tone alerted Margaret to something she couldn't quite identify. Sara continued, "I can speak some basic Hindi. I tend to consider my native tongue to be Nepali. I still think in it, sometimes. And, of course, Sherpali, but that's an offshoot of Nepali."

"Nepali? Say something in Nepali."

"Um." She picked up her glass and tipped it slightly toward Margaret. "Subhakamana."

"Bless you." Margaret offered a small smile. "Some kind of toast?"

"Yes, the Nepali version of 'cheers.'"

"Why do you consider Nepali your first language?"

Settling back into the leather seat, Sara took another sip of her drink and nodded. "I was born there, and it was what was spoken by everyone, including my parents, though clearly they taught me English too. Of course, they *taught* that to the villagers, so it was natural that I was in those classes. Their Nepali is, well, broken is probably the kindest way to put it. They tried, but growing up speaking it…" She shrugged. "It really helped me when I got my first job out of college."

"I can't imagine a job where you would need to have Nepali as a second language."

Sara sipped her wine and leaned back into the booth. "It helps when you're building sustainable farming enclaves in the outer regions of Nepal," she said rather dryly.

Somewhat chagrined, Margaret took another drink of her wine and then simply played with the glass. Were they having a normal conversation? It felt like it. Almost felt like a real date, even. They hadn't mentioned Stockton Industries or CoGS once. She frowned slightly as she recalled their opposing stances on the property.

Sara seemed to read her face. "Let's just have dinner," she suggested. "We have to eat, right? And we won't talk about the property, okay? We could just relax. We didn't leave our last conversation in a good place and I would like to have a better time tonight. All right?"

Suddenly, Margaret really wanted to have dinner with Sara Chandler. It was the politic thing to do, she told herself. Besides, she justified to herself, if she could get on Sara's good side, it would be that much easier to broker some kind of deal. And those tiny glimpses of some…thing…as they spoke intrigued her. Not that she wanted to be intrigued, but…

"Let's order," she said.

CHAPTER SEVEN

Sara stood just inside the doorway of the restaurant, her coat slung over one arm as she waited for Margaret to join her. She took a deep breath, enjoying the taste of the Sound, only a few blocks away, on the wind. At just past eight the sky was only beginning to color with evening light; the tops of the converted lofts surrounding her glowed in the setting sun. She smiled as Margaret waited for a couple to enter before joining her. "Everything okay?"

"Yes." Margaret paused, looking uncomfortable for a moment. "I, ah, was trying to get a copy of the menu to take with me."

"Oh, you should have said when we were inside. Since we did the pasta bar, I never really saw the menu."

Margaret shrugged into her light coat, then reached for Sara's. Automatically holding it for her. Sara slipped her arms into the sleeves, appreciating the gesture.

"It's not for me."

"Sorry?"

"The menu. It's for a friend."

"Ah." Not really understanding, Sara offered a smile, then held out her hand. "Well, thanks for a great dinner." She lifted her bag of boxed leftovers in salute.

Margaret pulled her attention from the restaurant door and looked down before taking Sara's hand in her own for a gentle handshake. "Thank *you*. I had a nice time."

Tipping her head, Sara studied her date. "Did you? I mean, *I* did, but…well, I know you were roped into this and then it was, well, *me*, and—"

The grip on her hand tightened, not painfully, but enough to stop her. "I had a really nice time, Sara. Really. I'm sorry about earlier. I just wasn't expecting…"

"Me."

"Yes."

"Well, to be honest, I'm not quite in a place to be set up for dates right now, but Mom insisted." They stepped aside as another couple approached the door and she smiled up at Margaret. "Moms, right?"

Margaret nodded. *Oh yes, moms indeed.*

"Well," Sara continued, "despite it being me, I'm glad you enjoyed dinner." She glanced at her watch and stepped back. "I need to get going if I'm going to catch the ferry."

"Ferry?" Margaret matched her stride to Sara's. "There's no ferry terminal around here."

"No." Sara pushed the button and they waited for traffic on Second to clear. "I'm headed toward Fauntleroy."

"You live in Port Orchard?"

"No. On Vashon Island." Together they stepped across the street and made their way along Bell. Sara stepped closer to Margaret to allow a large crowd of laughing twenty-somethings to pass and felt Margaret's hand settle into the small of her back. Even after they crossed the street, the hand remained and Sara found she liked it.

"Don't you find living on an island somewhat…limiting?"

"No. What do you mean?"

Margaret's strong face was puzzled. "Well, you have to schedule your life around other people's schedules—ferry times, wait times, et cetera. Don't you mind that?"

"No, not really. We have to do that in life anyway, don't we?"

"True. But..." Margaret shook her head. "Somehow I think it's more structured if you have to wait for things like transportation. You know?"

"I do." Sara stopped and tilted her chin toward the sign they now stood under. "This is my stop."

Margaret, who had continued on another two steps before realizing Sara was stopped, turned and looked around. "What?"

"My stop." Pointing to the sign that identified the space as a stop for the C Line of King County Transit, Sara smiled. "Or, more appropriately, my 'go.'"

"You're not taking the bus!"

Margaret's exclamation was more of an accusation than a question and Sara bristled. "Yes, actually, I am. I use public transit as much as possible."

"Don't you own a car?" Clearly the idea of someone *not* owning a car was as foreign to Margaret as walking on the moon.

"Of course I own a car," Sara snapped, working to keep her rising temper in check. Despite the pleasant evening they'd had, something about Margaret lit her normally long fuse like no other person she had ever met. They had hit a few topics this evening that had heated her temper, but she had simply changed the subject. On this, however, she wanted to make a point. "Just because I own a car does not mean I cannot or do not choose to take public transportation. It's better for the environment, better for the city, and, often, better for me." She reached into her pocket to make sure she had her Transit pass, then nodded to Margaret. "I guess this is good night, then."

Margaret glanced from Sara to the bus sign and back again before nodding. "I'm sorry, I just was surprised. I've got nothing against—"

"Quiet." Sara held up a hand and turned her face slightly away. She thought she had heard—

"I'm sorry?" The shock on Margaret's face at being interrupted was clear. "I was trying to—"

Sara's raised hand rose a bit higher, her other hand going to Margaret's arm, giving it a gentle squeeze. "Shh. I mean it." She turned her head the other way, listening over the sound of the evening traffic. "I thought I heard…wait. There it is again," she whispered.

Turning quickly, she walked quietly along Third, listening hard for the sound that had caught her attention. Another soft whimper, almost a sigh, brought her to an inset doorway mostly hidden from the lights of the brightening streetlights.

"Sara?" Margaret's voice was uncertain as she followed Sara.

"Over here," Sara called softly. "Be quiet, though. I think he's scared." She crouched down and called softly to the disheveled pile of fur curled against the doorframe. "Hey, baby, it's okay. Come on out, honey."

Keeping her voice low and smooth, she did her best to reassure the dog. Covered from head to tail in a tangled mass of matted hair and dirt, a pair of bright eyes peered out at her. As she talked, the dog's soft whining stopped and he eyed Sara hopefully. The tip of his tail lifted and fell and Sara felt her heart fall with it. She quickly opened her bag of leftovers and fished out a long, hollow noodle.

"Here you go, baby. Are you hungry?" The tip of the tail lifted and fell again and the dog's nose twitched. The bright eyes flicked from the noodle to Sara's face and back again.

Sara crooned to the dog again, keeping her voice low and comforting. She could feel Margaret behind her and was glad her companion remained silent. The dog was clearly frightened and just as clearly neglected. Sara's heart melted as a puff of warm air blew across her fingers before the noodle was swiped away by a rough tongue. "Good dog. Good. Here's another." Again the dog sniffed carefully and then gently took the food from Sara's fingers.

Behind her Margaret shifted. "Is it taking the food?"

"Yeah." Her knees beginning to protest from being so long in a crouch, Sara shifted and lost her balance, only to be caught as Margaret reached down and caught her shoulder. She held her steady as Sara repositioned and settled onto her knees, heedless of her clothes and the damp and dirty sidewalk. "Thanks."

"No problem." Margaret leaned down and looked over Sara's shoulder at the dirty stray. "Seems to like the pasta."

The dog looked up at the sound of her voice. Sara expected it to duck back, but the dog's tail thumped again, higher this time. He inched forward and looked up at Margaret, then back at Sara. Sara chuckled and handed him another noodle, then offered one to Margaret. "Here, you want a turn?"

Margaret shook her head and straightened. "Um, no. I don't really get dogs."

Sara's eyebrows shot up, but she didn't say anything as she fed the dog another small noodle.

"Looks like your bus is coming."

"Oh." Distressed, Sara looked up the street and saw that, indeed, her bus was about a block away. "Damn." She shook her head and reached into her pocket. "I'm going to have to call for a ride. I hope Lyft will let me take a dog in the car."

"Lyft?"

"Yes, unless you want to take the dog home with you?"

"Oh no." Margaret shook her head again. "Nope. No. No way. Not me." She held her hands up in something of a warding-off gesture.

"Wow. Okay. It's not like I'm asking you to adopt him. Her. Whatever. I just don't think I can take him on the bus." Shaking her head, Sara unlocked her phone and opened her Lyft app. The dog inched out a bit more, nose twitching toward the open box of pasta.

"Wait." Margaret stopped her with a hand on Sara's arm. "I'm parked not far from here. I can drive you."

"You can drive me? *And* the dog?"

Margaret looked past Sara to the dirty bundle of fur who now sat hopefully on the doorstep watching them both. She sighed and nodded. "Of course. I was going to offer you a ride anyway, but now…yeah. I'll go get my car." Without another word she turned and strode off, leaving Sara behind her, her mouth open.

"Well," she muttered as she turned back to the dog. "When she makes a decision, she certainly doesn't mess around, does she?" She moved back from the doorway, coaxing the dog out of the shadows. "Come on, big guy. Let's see the rest of you…and how much of you there is." Slowly, noodle by noodle, the dog stepped out of the doorway and closer to Sara. Bright golden-brown eyes followed every move Sara made, but she noticed the dog didn't spook or startle at the street noises going on around them. Its attention was wholly focused on Sara and her rapidly dwindling supply of dinner leftovers.

In the white light of the street lamps, mixed with the last of the day's sunlight, the dog's coat seemed to be a dark reddish brown, save for the gray of its paws and the tip of its tail. It looked almost as if someone had dipped all four feet and the tail into a bucket of gray paint no more than three inches deep.

When the last of the noodles were gone, Sara slowly stretched out a hand to let the dog sniff her palm. This time the tail rose and fell and kept moving, followed by a soft bump by the damp nose, a clear request for petting. With a smile, Sara obliged, trying not to think of what might be living in the matted fur beneath her fingers.

The last of the day's light was gone and Sara was about to give up on Margaret and call for a ride when bright headlights swept over them both. She squinted at the figure behind the wheel, her fingers unconsciously tightening on the dog's fur, the dog tensing right along with her. When Margaret stepped out from behind the wheel of the stylish, late-model Toyota, Sara and the dog both relaxed again.

"Sorry it took me a bit longer." Margaret came around the car and opened the back door. She stepped back and invited Sara in. "I assume you want to ride with your friend. I threw down an old blanket I had in the trunk."

Sara nodded and rose, wondering how she would coax the dog to join her in the car. Before she could consider any options, however, Margaret turned her attention to the dog. "Hey. We're going. You coming?" She snapped her fingers once and pointed to the open backseat. To Sara's astonishment, the dog gave one happy yip and jumped right in. Margaret turned to Sara and waved her forward. "You're up."

"Wow." Sara swallowed and nodded. "Okay. Yes. Fine." She got in and settled next to the dog, who was busily lapping up water from a large cup in the back cup holder. "Hey! I don't—"

"It's okay," said Margaret as she closed the door. Coming around the other side and sliding in behind the wheel, she continued, "I popped back into the restaurant and got them to give me the water. Figured it might be thirsty."

"Great idea." Sara settled back as Margaret pulled away from the curb. "You know where the ferry terminal is?"

"Yes."

"Great." Once they started moving, the dog stopped drinking and settled in next to Sara, who took the opportunity to check for important information. "I think your other passenger is a 'her,' by the way." She caught Margaret's eye in the mirror. "Unless some of the matted fur is hiding more than just dirt."

"Are you going to keep her?"

"I…yes. I would like to. I haven't had a dog for a long time and I miss it. It's sometimes a bit quieter out at my place than I would like. I'll get her checked for a chip and stuff at the vet. Probably after a bath."

"Or several," Margaret added dryly as she drove them out of downtown Seattle and down toward the ferry terminal that would take Sara to Vashon.

"Yeah. Probably." Sara petted the dog as they rode, enjoying the silky softness of her ears, despite the dirt and unmistakable smell of "street dog." "She's a pretty color. Kind of like a dusty sunset. Have you ever seen one?"

"A sunset? Of course. A 'dusty' one? Can't say that I have."

"Oh. They're something else." She leaned her head back on the leather headrest. "Not quite gold, not quite cream, with an overlay of reddish hue that makes the air seem to shimmer." Again she caught Margaret's eye and this time she smiled at the raised eyebrow. "Okay, maybe she's not that pretty…yet. But that's what I think of when I look at her fur."

Margaret pulled into the terminal, explaining to the ticket seller that she was simply dropping someone off. The man waved her through and she brought the car to a stop before the passenger shelter. "Here you go."

Sara opened the back door and stepped out, hoping the dog would follow without a leash. That might be a problem. "Come on, girl. Let's go home." With a glance at Margaret and a last tail thump, the dog hopped out and sat before Sara, looking up at her. "Good girl." She petted the dog's ears again. "Thanks again for the ride. I...we really appreciate it."

Margaret nodded. "Have fun with your new friend." She rolled down the front window as Sara closed the back door. "Thought of a name yet?"

Sara turned to look at the dog who sat so hopefully at her feet. The well-lit ferry terminal confirmed what she thought she had seen on the street. Despite the dirt and grime, there was a hint of dusty reddish fur around the eyes and ears. The approaching ferry let out a warning blast as she and the dog stepped away from the curb. Turning back to Margaret, she nodded. "No, but I'm sure it'll come to me."

* * *

Margaret's cell phone rang as she unlocked her apartment door. She dumped her purse and keys on the front table and glanced at the phone screen. Her mother. Of course it was.

How on earth did her mother know the exact minute she had returned from her blind date? Margaret might have suspected that her mother had put a GPS tracker on her phone or perhaps implanted a subcutaneous tracker when she was a teenager. If she asked her mother, of course, Carol would probably say something like "When you are in tune with the ebb and flow of the energy of time in the Universe, you sense the truth of what is happening" or some such nonsense.

Far better not to ask, Margaret decided.

"How was your date?" Carol asked.

"Fine."

"Fine? You can tell me more than that, Dusty."

"It was fine," Margaret repeated. She wasn't about to admit she'd met Sara before this evening. She could only imagine the barrage of cross-examination that would then commence.

"What did you do, dear?"

"The usual blind date activities," Margaret answered. "We had dinner. We talked about growing up and where we'd lived. She told me all about her parents trying to save the world, I told her all about my crazy, wacky, goat-cheese-making mother. As I said…the usual."

Her mother laughed as Margaret knew she would. She viewed all of Margaret's jibes as compliments.

"So what do you think?" Carol asked. "Did you feel a connection? Do you plan to see her again?"

"We didn't make another date, if that's what you're asking," Margaret said, lying by omission. That she would see Sara again, in one context or another, was a given.

"But you liked her," her mother said.

"Well, she's nice, but…I mean, she found a dog and took her home, for heaven's sake."

"A dog? At the restaurant?"

"No, outside as we were leaving. She looked homeless and hungry. She fed her her leftover dinner. She didn't have tags or a collar, so she decided she needed to adopt her on the spot. I had to take them to the ferry in my car."

"Wait. You took her to the ferry with a stray dog in your car?"

"Well, she couldn't very well take her home on the bus, could she?"

Margaret heard the defensiveness in her own voice.

Carol said, "Dusty, that's wonderful! She's a sweet and compassionate person, she loves animals. She must be an old soul! She will be perfect for you!"

"Mother, I'm not looking for a soul, old or otherwise."

"But you need someone, Dusty. She sounds lovely."

"Don't call me Dusty, Mother. And I don't need someone else to be happy. You're starting to sound like Mrs. Stein."

"I've always thought Mrs. Stein was a very wise woman," Carol said, her voice serene. "I'm very happy for you, dear."

"Are you really?" This conversation was worse than usual, Margaret thought.

Sarcasm was the least effective item in Margaret's "dealing with mother" toolbox, but she continued to employ it in case someday it actually worked.

"I am. You need to open your mind as well as your heart, dear. You're beginning to close yourself off from the possibilities the Universe is offering you. Sleep well, dear. Dream some happy dreams of the future."

CHAPTER EIGHT

"Oh, you *must* try this one, it's a new one."

Sandy smiled at her new friend and accepted the pale sliver of cheese, the third she had sampled today despite the fact that the cheeses she was making on her little farm were not exactly...palatable. She didn't have the heart to tell her that. Friendship was friendship, and she really didn't want to hurt Carol's feelings. She took a tiny nibble and smiled, despite its bitter and somewhat sour taste, quickly following up with a sip of her tea.

It was cozy in Carol's farm-stand shop. Outside, the rain fell in steady waves blown by the wind, occasionally rising and falling in pitch against the small glazed windows. In contrast to the weather, the inside of the little store was a welcome haven. A bright fire crackled in the tiny woodstove, throwing a surprising amount of heat while brightening up an otherwise gloomy afternoon. The firelight added just a bit of depth to the rough-hewn old oak walls, sending dancing shadows around the room while the scent of the burning wood flavored the air with a hint of the winter to come. Cans and jars, each covered or marked with the distinctive sketch of a goat and the logo of Carol's small farm, were arranged in varying heights on the rough shelving that lined the walls. Sandy pulled her stool closer to the counter, tugging it across a bump in the worn wooden floor. She rested her elbow on the counter and tucked her chin in her hand.

"So, any word from your girl on how the big date went?"

Carol rolled her eyes and sighed as she sliced another few slivers of cheese onto their shared plate. "Not likely. You?"

"No," Sandy sighed. "I've been really good, too, though it's been really hard. I haven't asked once, even though it's been three days."

"You're a better woman than I, Gunga Din. I've been grilling Dusty for the last two days."

"Dusty?"

"Margaret's first name. Sort of." Carol waved a hand in dismissal. "Forget I said it. She hates it when I use it."

A door slammed outside and Sandy smiled. "That'll be Sara, I told her I was coming out this way and she wanted to see your shop."

Before Carol could respond, Sara's voice carried into the shop. "Dusty, come on, honey. It's really coming down out here."

Carol and Sandy exchanged looks. Carol mouthed "Dusty?" and Sandy responded with "Honey?" Both women turned to face the door, anticipating the entrance of their daughters.

Sara, oblivious to the attention, stood inside the doorway, holding the door open for another minute. "C'mon, baby. It's too cold for you out there." She waited a moment, then said again, "Dusty, come *on*. We're letting out all of the heat!" She tossed her hood back and smiled apologetically inside. "Sorry, she's a bit stubborn."

"Oh, honey. You don't have to tell me." Carol turned away to pour two more cups of tea and kept chatting. "Though I'm a bit surprised you managed to get her to come out here."

"It wasn't hard," Sara said distractedly as she unzipped her dripping jacket and hung it on a peg near the door. "You just whisper the words, 'Wanna go for a ride?,' and she's game!"

Sandy sat at the counter in shock, staring at her daughter. Before she could say anything, a small sound caught her attention and Sara turned back to the door with a smile and opened it again.

"Finally!" She stepped back and held out a hand, stopping the large, dripping mass of dog from coming further into the shop. "Just a minute, young lady. I need to dry you off." She pulled a towel from her jacket pocket and began to rub down the dog, who was clearly enjoying the attention.

Carol, for her part, hadn't yet seen the newest addition to their little gathering. Still pouring out the tea, she continued her conversation as if uninterrupted. "Dusty always did like car rides. I remember this one time—" She turned around and stopped, shocked. "What is that?"

Sara spun around, looking behind her toward the door. She turned back to the counter. "What is what?"

"That?" Carol pointed to the dog, who turned her big golden eyes on her, barely visible from under the tuft of still-dripping fur.

"Oh, this. That's a dog. I mean, *she*. She's a dog." Sara straightened, her expression chagrined. "Sorry, I know it's rude to just bring her in, but Mom said you're good with animals, and…"

"No, it's fine." Carol shook her head. "But where's Dusty?"

Sara turned a puzzled gaze to her mother, then back to Carol. She gestured to the dog. "Um…right here."

"No, I meant—wait." She came around the counter and walked to Sara, holding out her hand. "Let's try this. Hi, I'm Carol. Welcome to the shop."

"Hi." Sara returned Carol's handshake. "I'm Sara and this is my new pal, Dusty." Sara turned to the dog. "Dust, say hi to Carol." The shaggy dog sat politely on the doormat and, after staring up at Carol for a long moment, lifted a paw in greeting.

"Well." Carol bent down and shook Dusty's paw. "Aren't you a sweetie? Nice to meet you, too." She straightened and waved Sara toward the counter. "So…'Dusty,' huh?"

"Yeah." Sara gave her mom a quick kiss on the cheek. "Hi, Mom." She settled onto the other stool and Dusty lay down at her feet. "I thought her fur looked kind of like a dusty sunset when we found her. You remember those, Mom?"

"We?" The older women latched onto the word quickly.

"Hm?" Sara took a quick sip of the tea Carol slid toward her. "Yes. Margaret and I found her the other night as we were walking to the bus stop. Well," she grinned at them both, "*I* found her and Margaret agreed we couldn't just leave her on a doorstep."

"And did you both name her?" Carol added more cheese and crackers to the plate on the counter, fighting back her smile.

"Nope, that was me. When I got her home and cleaned her up she was more of a reddish-gold, but she still reminded me of the sunsets in Nepal, so the name really seemed to fit."

Oblivious to the looks Carol and her mother exchanged, Sara bit into a cracker layered with cheese before Sandy could warn her. She immediately began coughing and gratefully accepted her teacup when her mother handed it to her. "Thanks." Eyes watering, she carefully set down the cracker and took another sip.

Windows rattled as a fierce gust of wind brought another, harder wave of rain. Carol frowned and stepped back from the counter and headed toward the back door. "I think it's time to add another log. I'll be right back."

Sandy watched her daughter sip her tea, one foot dangling from the stool to rub the dog's side. Dusty, for her part, seemed to enjoy the touch and lay as close to the stool as she could be, her gaze fixed on Sara. It was clear she had eyes for only one person. "So," Sandy ventured, "found her on your date, did you?"

"Mom."

"What?" Sandy raised her hands. "Just gathering information."

Before Sara could respond, Carol was back with an armload of wood. She waved Sara down when she started to get up to help. "No, no. Enjoy your tea with your mom. I've got this." She dumped the wood beside the old stove and, after tossing in two more logs, brushed off her jeans and shirt before heading into the back room once again.

The front door of the shop opened as another gust of wind hit, and this time it was Sara and her mom who watched the newcomer enter.

"Holy cow!" Margaret shrugged out of her long, waxed cotton coat. "It might be time to build that ark, Mom!" She hung her jacket on the peg next to where Sara's raincoat was still dripping and turned, stopping in surprise.

"Sara?"

"Hey!" Sara's smile was wide and bright, and Sandy simply watched. Her quiet, controlled Sara was grinning at the newcomer. She looked from Sara to the other woman and put two and two together. Sandy reached around Sara as Margaret moved closer and held out a hand. "Hi, I'm Sandy, Sara's mom." She liked the look of Margaret and appreciated the strong, firm handshake. She seemed...intense. Sandy was afraid for a moment she had made a mistake encouraging Sara to meet her, then Margaret glanced at Sara and then back to Sandy and smiled. The smile lit up Margaret's face and Sandy relaxed.

"Hi. Margaret Winters."

"I'll be right out," Carol called from the back. "I've got just the thing here for Dusty."

Margaret groaned, but so quietly Sandy was sure she was the only one who heard it. "Mom, *please*. I've asked you—"

"Oh!" Carol emerged from her storeroom and came around the counter. "Honey, I didn't know you were here. Just a sec." She quickly kissed her daughter's cheek, then bent down to lay a huge, meaty bone before the dog. "Here you go, Dusty," she said, shooting her daughter a wicked grin.

Margaret looked from her mother to the dog and then up at Sara. "Dusty?" she said quietly.

"Yep." Absentmindedly Sara reached again for another cheese sample but caught the look her mother sent and instead picked up her tea.

Margaret glanced suspiciously at her mother and Sandy bit back a smile. "How did you pick the name?"

"You weren't around for the bath. Or...*baths*, plural. But, once the dirt came off, that lovely dusty gold color came out and it just seemed to fit."

Margaret looked again from Sara to her mom but said nothing.

For her part, Carol just grinned. "Tea? I just made a fresh pot. And there's new cheese." Carol handed her daughter a cracker topped with a freshly cut slice of white cheese, then ducked back down behind the counter. "Let me get another plate."

Margaret settled onto the empty stool next to Sara, bumping her hand against the counter as she did so, causing the cheese to bounce off the cracker and drop to the floor. The three seated women watched as Dusty lifted her head from the bone to sniff delicately at the white crumbly gift from above. She gave it a tiny lick, then another before letting out a loud sneeze. She looked up at Margaret, her gaze clearly accusatory, then went back to her bone. Margaret glared back at the dog while Sara and Sandy muffled giggles.

Carol emerged from behind the counter, plates in hand. She leaned over the counter to look at the dog. "Oh dear. I hope she's not getting a cold."

* * *

"I think the rain's finally let up," Margaret said, putting down her empty teacup with a clatter. "I probably need to head home."

"Dusty and I will walk you out," Sara said. "Come on, girl."

Sandy finished her tea and excused herself, heading toward the restroom. "I'll be back in a minute, no need to wait."

"Just a sec," Carol said. "I'm sending cheese home with all of you. It'll just take me a second to wrap it up."

"No, really, Carol, you don't need to…" Sara said.

"Oh, no, I don't mind at all. I'll be back in a minute."

She disappeared into the back. Margaret looked sadly at Sara and said, "That never works."

"What never works?"

"There is no hint, insinuation, or suggestion that you can make that will have an impact on my mother. If you would perhaps not like to have goat cheese every day of your life, that will not prevent my mother from imposing cheese on you for every occasion. You are trapped. Surrender to your fate and take the cheese to work. Maybe a coworker will develop a fondness for it."

"Did that work for you?"

"Not yet. I have not given up hope."

Sara laughed. She had a nice laugh, from the belly, with a nice throaty sound. On impulse, Margaret asked, "Would you like to have coffee tomorrow? I have some errands and we could meet at that place by Pike Place Market. What's it called?"

"Three Girls Bakery? Sure, they have good coffee and great muffins."

"Oh, I was thinking of Storyville, but—"

"No, that's great. Let's meet there. It's probably quieter than Three Girls."

"How's their goat cheese?"

"Which place?"

"Either."

Sara cocked her head in thought. "Never seen any on the menu at Three Girls, no idea about Storyville. Maybe we could bring our own?"

"Let's skip it. Will two o'clock work?"

"I'll look forward to it."

Carol returned with three brown paper-wrapped packages. She set one aside and handed Margaret and Sara each their own bags. "You'll love this. It's got basil and some garlic. I call it nanny goat pesto."

Oh, joy. "Thanks, Mom."

Sara, her hands full of cheese and dog leash, shrugged into her jacket and smiled at Margaret's mother. "Yes, thanks, Carol. I can hardly wait."

Margaret merely raised an eyebrow as she held the door open for Sara, whispering under her breath as they slipped out, "Your nose looks a little long, Pinocchio."

CHAPTER NINE

"I don't suppose I could interest you in a nice wedge of goat cheese," Margaret said to Mrs. Stein.

"No, thank you, dear. I'm trying to clean out everything, pantry and closets and refrigerator."

Margaret sipped at her jasmine tea, trying to hide her unhappiness. She didn't like being reminded of Mrs. Stein's impending departure. She didn't know what she was going to do with herself on Saturday mornings after she left.

Mrs. Stein carefully examined the shortbread cookies arranged on the plate between them. She selected one, plucking it up between two manicured fingers, and brought it delicately to her lips for a nibble.

She sighed.

"I'm going to miss these," she said wistfully. "And our little chats, of course."

"Yes," Margaret agreed. "I will, too. You've been a good friend to me."

Mrs. Stein smiled.

"Thank you, my dear. It's always nice to have some young people in your life as you get older. Keeps your perspective fresh. So, tell me. How is it going with your new friend?"

Margaret hadn't told her much about Sara, since she didn't want Mrs. Stein to proceed down the path Carol had taken. One matchmaker in her life was enough for Margaret.

"We're fine," Margaret said cautiously. "It's early yet."

"Yes, dear. But as you know, if things are right, relationships can proceed very quickly."

"You were engaged to George in just a few months after your first date, weren't you?" Margaret asked.

"That's right. I think I knew by the time he took me home that first evening. He was everything I'd been looking for and I didn't even know it."

Was that what Margaret had been doing? Looking for someone without even knowing it?

That was ridiculous, Margaret decided. She knew her own mind, of course. She knew what she wanted from life. Not a romantic relationship, not while she was trying to climb the local government power ladder.

And certainly not with Sara Chandler.

She was getting tired of going round and round in her head about Sara. When she was with her, she felt, well, different. Better, more lighthearted. But the Pacific Rim project loomed like a wall between them, a wall Margaret couldn't find a way around.

Mrs. Stein said, "You're not eating your cookies, dear."

Margaret picked up a shortbread.

"Why are these so good?" she asked through a mouthful of crumbs.

Mrs. Stein smiled.

"Butter," she answered. "We've grown so accustomed to substitutes that when we taste the real thing it's like nectar. The first thing I need to do after I find a new bridge club is to find a good bakery. Will you come and visit me, Margaret?"

Margaret swallowed against the lump in her throat that wasn't a bite of cookie.

"Of course I will."

"Good. And I expect you to bring your new girlfriend with you. I'd like to meet the woman that makes you stare off into space instead of eating your cookies. Whatever else you've done, my dear, you've never failed to enjoy your sweets."

* * *

Sara pulled open the glass doors of the high-end coffee shop and pulled off her sunglasses. She frowned as she approached the huge sleekly curved bar. There was no menu in sight. While she was normally not a shy person, the curved chrome and wood edifice was intimidating, as was the very hip-looking young man behind the bar, right down to the perfectly sculpted curl of hair that fell gracefully over one eye.

"Hi, first time here?"

"Yes. I'm meeting someone, but she's running a bit late."

"Welcome. We've got some free samples, and here's the menu if you would like to take some time. I'm here when you have questions or are ready to order."

Sara took the menu and scanned the room. The room's subtle lighting was enhanced by the huge half-circle mullioned windows that filled the wall adjacent to the bar. Light spilled over the wood floors, warming them to a light chocolate. The wall opposite the bar was lined with comfortably worn leather chairs and couches framing a large fireplace. Small wood tables were scattered throughout, some with old books on them, others with board games or a puzzle. Walls covered in artfully arranged "distressed" wood provided a nice contrast to the old brick that framed the large windows, giving the place that pub-like feel with an upscale flare. The scents of wood, coffee, tea, and lovely baked goods added the final touch. Sara immediately relaxed. Despite the overpowering bar that fairly screamed "overproduced and trendy" when you first came in, the rest of the place simply said, "relax and have a seat." It was an interesting juxtaposition.

Settling into the corner of the large L-shaped brown leather couch, Sara set the menu aside, deciding she would wait for Margaret. This was, after all, Margaret's choice, so she might have some recommendations. She rested her arm on the back of the couch and set her chin on her arm, content to watch the people scurrying in and out of Pike Place Market.

Tourists were the easiest to spot—backpacks, cameras, and umbrellas. No Washington native ever carried an umbrella; it was nearly a point of pride. Locals could also be spotted wearing the business attire of the Pacific Northwest. For men it was tan slacks, fitted, a button-down shirt with a wide plaid, and a navy jacket or blazer held in place by a cross-body messenger bag of canvas or leather. For women it was long-legged black or blue trousers, a loose-fitting stylish white or tan tee covered by a mid-thigh length sweater or coat, and an oversized shoulder bag.

It was funny, she thought, as she counted yet another man striding by in his brown loafers and the uniform of the day. For a city that prided itself on its individual, independent spirit, nearly everyone wore the same thing.

Sara glanced down at her own worn blue jeans, sneaker-clad feet, and soft cotton button-down and shrugged. She seemed to be bucking the norm, but she was used to that. She looked up with a smile as Margaret appeared around the corner of the coffee bar, pulling off her own sunglasses. Margaret, too, was "out of uniform," as it were. In fact, Sara realized, Margaret was wearing the men's "uniform" and far better than most of the men were!

"Hey, sorry I'm late." She tossed her leather satchel and sunglasses on the low table before the couch and sat down with a sigh. She stretched her neck back and let her head fall onto the couch cushions, her eyes closed.

"You're not late, no worries." Sara tilted her head. "Everything okay? You seem…stressed."

Margaret shook her head, then sat up. "No, things are fine. It's just work." She looked around and spotted the menu on the cushions between them. "I'm starved."

Recognizing the diversion for what it was, Sara pointed with her chin toward the menu. "Me, too. What's good?"

"Everything."

"Come on."

"No." Margaret looked up and held Sara's gaze. "I mean it. Everything. I've never had anything here that was less than exceptional."

"Wow, with a recommendation like that…" Sara took back the menu from Margaret. "I was thinking of having the Chai tea, just a cup. I can't decide on food. It all smells and looks amazing." She leaned forward to get out of the corner of the couch, but Margaret stopped her.

"I'll get it, my treat." She stood, then turned back to Sara. "Anything in it? Do you trust me to order you some food?"

"Nothing in the tea and…" She paused and smiled up at Margaret. "Sure, surprise me. But, um, no nuts. I'm allergic."

Margaret's eyes widened. "Oh, good to know."

Sara watched as Margaret strode to the bar. Strode. The woman didn't *walk*, she took determined *strides*. She wondered if that was something she did on purpose or just a natural thing. Margaret and the barista chatted while she ordered, then she laughed at something the man said, her rich, rolling laugh carrying back to Sara. Not loud or obnoxious, but warm and inviting. She liked that laugh, Sara realized. Liked the rich depth of Margaret's voice, a depth matched by her expressive face and eyes, two things that never failed to capture Sara's attention.

When she came back, she held a couple of plates and two forks. She set the plate down and grinned at Sara. "Life's short, let's start with dessert."

Centered on the plates was a large rolled and perfectly browned pastry covered in a golden glaze, shiny crystals of… "Is that sea salt on there?" Sara looked up from her study to Margaret.

With a grin, Margaret offered her a fork. "Oh, yes. Yes it is."

Taking the fork, Sara cut carefully into the pastry and sighed as a small puddle of caramel oozed out of the center. "Oh, no way."

"Mmph." Margaret was enjoying her own taste. "Way."

Sara gently cut off and collected a piece and popped it into her mouth. The combination of pastry and caramel balanced by the tiny bite of sea salt was sensational and she simply closed her eyes to savor it.

"Well?"

"Shh," she muttered over her still-melting bite. "Shh. I'm having a moment."

Margaret's warm chuckle added to that moment and Sara absorbed the sound as well as the sensations on her tongue and tied them together. A thrilling combination, indeed.

* * *

Sara dabbed at her eyes and gasped for breath, one hand on a side already aching from laughing. "You're making that up!"

"I swear, right in front of the judge." Margaret held up her hand as if she were taking an oath.

Shaking her head as she spooned up the last of her tomato soup, Sara chuckled again. They had spent the last hour trading work stories and Margaret's last one had nearly caused soup to gush from Sara's nose. She glanced at her watch and grimaced, hating to end their time together but knowing she had to get back to her own office. "I hate to do this, but—"

Margaret nodded. "I know, me too."

Sara drank the last of her tea and fidgeted with her napkin. "This place is great, thanks."

"Yeah, I found it not long after I moved here. The bar's a little…well, you saw it."

They shared a laugh, Sara glancing again at the imposing bar. "Well, the food makes up for it." She fidgeted again with her napkin again before setting it down. "I had a nice time, again. Thanks for this."

"You sound surprised." Margaret's gaze was direct and she had one eyebrow raised.

"Well, I figured you were blindsided on that blind date and were on your best behavior. Then, Dusty and I ran into you at your mom's store, and again, best behavior, right?" She shrugged.

"Not really, but okay." Margaret's tone had cooled somewhat.

"So, this...today." Sara looked around the room, her gaze encompassing the space and the little corner where they had spent the last hour laughing and talking. "It's just—when we met up in the rooftop garden and that phone call. That's more in line with what I had, um, heard of you."

"What you'd...heard...of me."

Now her tone was nearly flat, and Sara was sad to note that the light of good humor was mostly gone from her eyes. "Well, yes. After you came to see me in the garden, I did some checking and I had heard that you can be kind of...well, a cold fish."

The flicker passed so quickly over Margaret's face that Sara would've missed it if she hadn't been watching for it. "I can be a bit of a shark—when it comes to work, I mean."

"Sorry," Sara offered. "Didn't mean to hit a nerve."

"You didn't." Margaret's reply was sharp, some of the earlier warmth gone from her voice. She turned away to stare out of the window, sipping her coffee.

Sara bit her lip, then reached out and laid her hand over Margaret's. "I did, and I'm sorry. For what it's worth, I don't see you that way."

Margaret leaned back and gave Sara an appraising look.

"You know what? I am a realist. I grew up with a mother who spent her life in la-la land, with rainbows and unicorns. I pride myself on living in the real world facing real problems. I see what needs to be done and I do it. If that's being a shark, okay. But I'm not doing it for myself. I want a better city."

"Don't you think that's what I want, too?" Sara asked.

"I don't know," Margaret admitted. "What do you want?"

Sara gazed at her for a moment. There were dark gold flecks of color in Margaret's dark eyes she hadn't noticed before. What did she want? The answer shook her. *Maybe it's you.*

CHAPTER TEN

Sara rolled her car into the driveway behind the old pickup truck and set the brake. Tipping her head to rub it against Dusty's muzzle, she reached around and gave the dog a good scratching behind her ear. "Okay, girl. You're in the shade, the windows are halfway down, the back window is open, you have water, and I won't be long."

Dusty gave a gusty sigh and rested her head on Sara's shoulder, pleading with her large golden eyes and making her laugh. "Oh, come on…I can't just let you wander around. I have no idea if she would like that." She met the dog's gaze in the rearview mirror and shook her head. "And stop looking at me like that!"

Dusty licked her ear, gave a soft, wet huff, then turned her back on Sara and curled up onto the bed that took up most of the back of Sara's little SUV.

Sara shook her head again, gave the dog a last pat, and opened the door. Carol had invited her to tour the farm, and Sara was eager to see what it was about. Carol's shop had been impressive, and Sara wondered if there were some way the people who would be building community gardens in the new downtown Seattle site could either make their own co-op store or perhaps partner with Carol. Either way, she really wanted to see how Carol did things. She also *really* didn't want to try any new cheeses. Margaret had been right. She had gotten home and tried what Carol had so sweetly packed up for her. Sara felt her lips puckering at just the memory of the bitter, almost *angry* cheeses. It was an experience she was loathe to repeat.

Gravel crunched under her feet as she walked the neatly trimmed pathways between small buildings. Farm smells, rich and redolent with earthy scents, rode the slight breeze, reminding her of her childhood. She had loved growing up in Nepal, so close to the land, to the people. Carol's farm brought a lot of those memories back. Of course Carol didn't have yak wandering loose alongside chickens, dogs, children, and horses, but the smells were the same. Sara closed her eyes and took in a slow, deep breath. The scents were so achingly familiar that she half-expected to turn a corner and find her auntie, or *cācī*, Shanti, in her colorful *kurta-suruwal* sari pants, hunkered down, one bare and dusty foot keeping her *charkha*, her miniature spinning wheel, moving while her hands pulled and twisted the fluffy cloud of yak *khulu*, the finest, softest fiber from the yak, into silky, fine yarn.

"Sara?" Carol's soft voice pulled her from her memories, and Sara opened her eyes to find Carol standing before her, a concerned and puzzled expression on her face.

"Hi, Carol." Sara brushed a hand over her eyes, adjusting her sunglasses as she did so. She was surprised by the wave of homesickness. Her recent assignment had been in India, but it wasn't Nepal. While she had been gone from that country for years, it would always be a sort of home for her.

"Are you okay, dear?"

Smiling, Sara returned Carol's hug of greeting. "Yes, sorry. You caught me just..." She looked around and smiled. "Just enjoying the sights and smells."

Carol's eyebrows rose as she stepped back. "Huh. Most people don't enjoy the smelly part."

"Smells like good food and health to me."

"I always thought so. I pretty much grew up here. This place belonged to my great-aunt Shirley." Carol smiled and waved her hand vaguely to encompass the lush green fields dotted with buildings and neatly delineated pastures and enclosures. "I ran wild here, woman and girl, until I ran even further." She shrugged. "Ah well, youth. The things we do…" She led Sara toward the nearest building. "Your mom said you grew up in, oh, where was it?"

"Nepal. Until I was thirteen."

"Your family has lived such an interesting life. Were you in Kathmandu? I've always wanted to go there."

Sara smiled. Everyone always asked that. "No, in the small village of Khartuwa. It's a village in the Sitalpati V.D.C. Ward of Sankhuwasabha District, in the Kosi Zone of northeastern Nepal."

Carol stopped and stared, her mouth dropping open slightly. "The, um, Veedee of the ah…" she said faintly.

Sara laughed. "Sorry, I'm so used to rattling that off. Khartuwa is a very small village in a Village Development Council, or Vee Dee Cee," she spelled out the letters. "That's sort of like a, hmm…a county here, I guess. The Sankhuwasabha District would be roughly the equivalent of a state, and the Kosi Zone is, I guess, a region."

"Oh. Sure. Of course." Shaking her head, Carol smiled at Sara. "How did someone who grew up in the VDC of Sankawashing kosher zones of Nepal end up with a name like Sara Chandler? Or do you have a Nepalese name?"

"Nepali, or, more correctly to us, Khas Kura." Sara grinned at the expression on Carol's face. "Or, *really* correctly, it would be Sherpali, but that's taking things a bit far."

"Sherpali?" As they talked, Carol led them from one barn to the next. The first contained mostly tools and equipment, the second a large and empty space with newly washed concrete floors and bays with hoses and large channels set into the concrete. "This is the shearing barn for our sheep. We don't have many, but we like to make them work for their food." She waved Sara through a small door that led to a covered corridor, then down through another door. "I didn't know that Sherpa had their own language."

Nodding, Sara kept up, glad she had put on her old Wellies for this trip. The barn floors were either damp or littered with straw and she had noticed that the pens were quite muddy.

"Sherpali is mainly spoken, not written, and is really derived from the Tibetan language. The village where I was born is the Sherpa region of Nepal and everyone there speaks Sherpali, Nepali, or Tibetan, or some mixture of all three." She felt color creep up on her cheeks and ducked her head. "Sorry, I could talk about this stuff all day. Language and etymology are kind of hobbies of mine."

"Don't apologize, dear. I asked." Carol's smile, and her interest, were genuine.

Sara nodded. "You did. Okay, so…my name." She leaned against the low half-door and watched as Carol filled buckets with feed, measuring out equal amounts of pellets with small, green grains and adding powder from various bottles arranged on the shelves. "My full name is Sarasvati Noelani Chandler."

"Wow, that's quite the mouthful." Carol smiled over her shoulder at Sara. "Am I being too 'American' if I ask if the names have some meaning or translation?"

Laughing, Sara shook her head. "Of course not. Do you want the whole spiel or just the name stuff?"

"Ohh, there's a spiel?" Carol grinned as she washed her hands. "Let's hear it. I love this stuff."

Sensing a kindred spirit, Sara grinned back. "Okay. We're not Hindu, but we followed the culture in the village. Eleven days after I was born, and after combining my birth details and composing a horoscope for me, the village priest came to our home to perform the *nwaran*, the naming ceremony. He told my dad, my *baba*, who, as the elder of our family, announced my name to everyone. Most Nepali names come from Sanskrit or Pali, and mine is one of the derivations of the Sanskrit 'Saraswati,' a Hindu river goddess. Her name means 'essence of being' or 'bringer of water,' depending on which translation you read. Noelani is Hawaiian and means 'mist of heaven.' I think my mom was on a water kick."

"I do sense a theme, and that's quite the spiel."

"Tell me about it. Anyway, I'm glad my mom kept with the western tradition when doing the middle name. Had the priest had his say, it would have likely been 'Himalaya.'"

Laughing, Carol handed Sara two buckets and hefted two more of her own. "You're kidding!"

"No, all of our names have some significance and meaning, and many of my friends' names reflected where we lived. They love to celebrate the beauty and tranquility of the place. I'm not sure I could go through life with the middle name of 'snow-capped mountains.'"

Carol's laughter echoed in the empty building as she led the way back out through the corridor, but this time turned to the right and stopped to open a pen. "I guess when it comes to names, I really have no room to talk."

Before she could elaborate, they had reached the baby goat pen. She smiled at Sara's delighted gasp and stepped back to let her enter, then carefully looped the strap to secure the metal gate. "Well, Saras…something-something Chandler, meet the kids. Literally."

She dumped both of her buckets into feed troughs and then relieved Sara of her two, doing the same for the troughs on the far side, freeing Sara to kneel down as the baby goats skipped and danced around them both.

The two women chatted amiably as the small kids cavorted around them, hopping and skipping, blithely flinging their bodies into the air and each other. Sara got one or two to nibble feed pellets from the palm of her hand while Carol told her how the farm worked. The cheese-making enterprise was her newest venture and she was really excited about it. Sara, in turn, plied her with questions about the store's operation, getting some good ideas for her own project.

Finally, after about fifteen minutes, Carol rose and offered a hand to Sara. "Let's head over to the other barn. You can meet the teenagers."

Reluctantly Sara rose and brushed the dust and straw from her jeans, watching the little animals continue to play. She followed Carol from the pen, secured the gate, and the two crossed the yard and entered the larger of the four barns set around the square.

"I really appreciate you taking me around like this," she said as they moved through the larger barn and into a wider, grassier field than the smaller pen they had just left.

Carol grabbed a pitchfork as they passed a large pile of hay and began forking it into racks tied into the fence rails. "It is my pleasure, dear." The larger kids came bounding across the field, jostling and shoving one another in an effort to reach hayracks Carol was filling with bright green hay.

"Now, down here are the bigger kids. They're around six months old. I'll warn you, they may look cute, but they can be pushy. Stand your ground."

"Okay." The noise was tremendous, and Sara could only imagine Dusty's reaction to the knee-high, energetic kid-goats. She'd probably try to herd them, or roll over and then let them play with her. "It's a good thing I left Dusty in the car, I think."

"Is she okay?"

"I'm sure she is. I left the windows mostly open, and the back has a mesh over it, so she's got lots of air.

Carol, a long hose in one hand and a small bucket in another, was sluicing out the water trough, clearly only half listening. "Oh, that's good." She stepped back and let the water arc into the trough, splashing nearby kids into more spurts of energetic skips and spins. Some attempted to catch the water as it fell, only to sneeze as they inhaled it.

Sara was as entertained by the "teenagers" as she had been by the babies in the other pen. They skipped and hopped all around her, a few nuzzling and butting her pockets, one attempting to chew the edge of her green Wellies. She accepted a handful of pellets from Carol and tried to be fair in her feeding, but the goats kept milling and butting her hands, sending pellets flying. She laughed as one guy practically climbed into her lap. Carol re-coiled the hose and settled onto the hay bale beside her and fed a few of the little ones herself. She pointed out the names of each one and showed Sara where they most loved to be scratched.

It surprised Sara how much she enjoyed sitting in the goat pen, the late-afternoon sunlight slanting along the dust churned up by the playful kids. It reminded her again of Nepal, of being a little girl and watching her *baba* and the other men herding the goats there into pens. The scent of the sun-warmed hay added to the color of the afternoon and she closed her eyes and soaked in the feeling.

"Are you sure you're okay, my dear?"

Sara opened her eyes to meet Carol's concerned gaze. "Yes, I'm great. Really great." She breathed in again and grinned at Carol. "This really reminds me so much of how I grew up, the goats, the sun and hay, the smells. All of it." She shrugged. "Sometimes I miss it. Things were so simple there. And then."

"They usually seem that way." Carol patted Sara's knee. "So, you like the kids, then?"

"They are absolutely charming. Dusty would love to play with them."

"She used to." Carol stood. "Not so much anymore." She carefully opened the gate so they could slip out, and as she latched it again, she glanced back toward the driveway. "Must be an important call."

Confused, Sara stood and brushed off her jeans, then followed Carol's gaze. She didn't see anything unusual. Puzzled, she tilted her head. Maybe she had misheard. "I'm sorry, do you need to make a call?"

Carol shook her head and waved Sara toward the larger of the two barns. "Dusty. In the car. I figured it was a phone call."

Utterly baffled, Sara stopped. "Carol, are you okay?"

"Of course I am, dear. Why?"

Sara looked closely at Carol and wondered if the woman was just messing with her. Then she thought of Devery and a hot spike of fear shot through her. It had started just like this. One minute they were having a normal conversation and the next...*snap!* What if Margaret's mother were having the same sort of thing? Or a brain hiccup or...

"Sara, dear, are you okay?" Carol stepped close and put her hand on Sara's arm.

"Me?" Sara shook her head. "I'm trying to figure out why you think Dusty would...or could...make a phone call."

"I assume for the same reason—and by the same means—anyone would."

Oh God. What were you supposed to ask a stroke victim? FARTS? No, of course not. FATS? No....FAST! She looked carefully at Carol's face, spying as she did so the cell phone riding in the pocket of the short-sleeve button-down she was wearing. She grabbed it, eliciting a squawk from Carol. Did this area even have EMS? Margaret. She would call Margaret...if she could figure out which number was hers.

She examined Carol's face again; she didn't see any drooping. What the hell came next? What did the A stand for? Screw it.

"Okay, okay. It'll be okay." She grasped the hand Carol had on her arm and gripped her fingers tightly as she led them both to the low stone bench beneath the willow. "Carol, do you know what day it is?"

"Of course I do. You're awfully pale, all of a sudden, dear. Are you sure you're okay?"

"I'm fine, I'm fine. Just a second." She flipped the cover of the phone over and cursed as the phone sailed from her nervous fingers.

"I'll get it."

"No!" Sara jumped up and grabbed the phone, wiping the face off on her jeans.

"Maybe you should have Dusty drive you home."

"Carol," Sara spoke slowly, gently. "Dusty can't drive me home. Remember? Dusty is a dog."

"What does that have to do with anything?"

Carol's confused look nearly broke Sara's heart. She changed her mind about calling Margaret and instead simply hit the emergency call button. As the call connected, she held Carol's hand tightly in hers and hoped she remembered the address of the farm correctly. "Carol, honey, dogs can't drive."

"I know that!"

Sara held up a hand and responded to the questions the dispatcher asked her.

"Yes, hi." She leaned past Carol and spotted the mailbox. Squinting, she rattled off the address for the woman, and then, her hand still wrapped around Carol's, she began describing what she was seeing. "Yes, sixty-something woman, very fit. I think she's having a stroke. Yes. Yes. I'm with her now."

"I'm not having a stroke!"

"Let's let them decide that, Carol."

"Oh, for goodness' sake!" Carol yanked her hand from Sara's and strode away, heading for the driveway.

"Where are you going?" Sara jumped up and followed, still talking to the dispatcher. "Yes, I'll keep her calm. Or I'll try. Just tell them to hurry, please." She caught up with Carol and tried to step in front of her, only to dodge as Carol pivoted around her and kept going. "Carol, where are you going?"

"To get Dusty. There's clearly something wrong with you and she can help."

"Carol!" Before Sara could say another word, Carol yanked open the passenger door of Sara's car, leaned in, then…simply dropped into the empty front seat.

When Sara sprinted around the car, she found Carol sitting sideways on the passenger seat, her elbows on her knees, her face cupped in her hands, and her shoulders shaking. Sick at heart, memories of Devery's stroke and its aftermath still so fresh, Sara stepped slowly forward and laid a gentle hand on the older woman's shoulders. What the hell was she going to tell Margaret? *Oh, god. Margaret.* She had to call her. What could she say?

As she squatted down in front of Carol, she could hear the distant wail of sirens. *Oh, thank god.* Dusty stood, her head between the two front seats, nuzzling the back of Carol's neck.

"Carol?" She set the phone down, laid her hands on Carol's knees, and gently squeezed. "Carol," she said softly. "It's okay. We can—" She stopped. Carol had slid her hands aside and she was…laughing. Laughing! Sara shook her head. "What's…are you…"

"Oh!" Carol wiped her eyes, her laughter uncontained. "Oh, oh, my!"

She was simply incomprehensible with laughter. Sara was at a complete loss. She had never heard of someone having a stroke and then a laughter attack. Or was this something else? Dusty was wiggling her way between the seats now, frantically licking Carol's ears and neck, her tongue wagging wildly at the unexpected visitors. Sara tried to push her back, but Carol shook her head and laughed even harder.

CHAPTER ELEVEN

Tucked into a corner booth at Storyville, Sara kept her eyes closed as she forced her still-tense body to relax. What an afternoon. It had taken both Sara and Carol talking with both medics more than a half hour to convince them that *neither* woman was having a stroke. It had taken Carol nearly that long to stop chuckling, and even after the paramedics left, she had occasionally let one slip.

While Sara could see the humor of it, *now*, she was still a bit jittery inside, her nerves still singing. It had been too much, too close, too similar. The afternoon sun slanted through the large half-circle windows, warming her shoulders, and sending her mind back to that wonderful, then horrible, afternoon.

Sara stretched out on the woven blanket, arms tucked behind her head, bare feet crossed at the ankle, her silken shirt and sari pants fluttering in the gentle breeze. It was one of those glorious, brilliant afternoons of sunshine interrupted by a few large, fluffy clouds chasing each other across the azure sky. The wind carried with it the scent of freshly turned earth, of farm and animals, the distant laughter of children. A perfect end to a perfect day.

The thump of someone landing hard on her blanket jarred her from her relaxation, and Sara sat up, slightly irritated. Devery always did that. Had to "announce" her presence in some way. Banging open a door, hopping onto a boat to make it shake and bob, throwing her body down in a dramatic way. Sara raised herself up onto her elbows, then lifted a hand to shade her eyes. "Back from your walk already?"

Devery nodded, rubbing a hand across her forehead. "Yeah. Headache."

Sara sat up all the way and reached into the small cooler, pulling out a bottle of water and handing it over. "Here. Maybe you got overheated."

Nodding again, but carefully, Devery opened the bottle. "Maybe. Didn't feel like it. Actually, I was feeling great and—" She stopped, her expression frozen, then she looked around, locked eyes with Sara, and simply collapsed.

"Dev!" Sara reached out and pulled Devery into her arms, shaking her, trying to wake her. "Dev! Devery! Wake up, honey. Wake up!"

Later she could not have told anyone how she got them both down to the village. The ride into the clinic at Zhangmu was a blur, as was the time spent waiting for the medical airlift to Kathmandu. She wouldn't, couldn't forget the sounds of that flight, however. Hearing the medic calling to Devery again and again, trying to get a response. The one time she had looked back, she wished she hadn't. The image of Dev's head thrown back, her hands fisted and curling in, the medic kneeling next to her, Dev's shirt open, the medic rubbing her knuckles hard against her chest, hard enough to leave dark red marks.

Nothing. No response.

Sara shuddered at the memory, the motion jolting her from the half-doze she had been in. She looked around, startled to find Margaret sitting quietly beside her, her eyes intent on her face. She rubbed her eyes, then sat up completely. "Margaret?"

"Hi." Margaret's soft greeting was low and warm. She reached down and handed Sara a steaming mug. "Here, you look like you could use this."

Automatically reaching for the mug, Sara blinked, trying to clear her head. "Thanks. How did you find me?" She took a deep breath, savoring the steam rising from the mug, grateful for the gesture.

"Mom called." A small smile slid across her face. "When she told me you said you were heading back into town, I tried your office first. They said you had taken a coffee break, so I took a chance. Mom said there had been some confusion out at the farm. She gave me the rundown." The smile turned into a quiet chuckle.

"Yeah," Sara said weakly. "It was funny." She worked up a small smile and tried to find the humor in the situation. It *had* been funny, in a way—once Carol had stopped laughing long enough to explain the mix-up. She had managed to leave the farm and get back to her office with Dusty without incident, but after sitting at her desk for a few minutes, the memories just kept coming. With Dusty asleep in her office, Sara had taken a much-needed break to collect herself and ended up at the coffee shop Margaret had introduced to her.

Margaret, her eyes on her own drink, chuckled again. "Dogs can't drive," she quoted Sara's own words back to her and looked up to share the joke. When she saw Sara's face, however, all trace of laughter fled. "Hey, oh, hey. Sara, I'm sorry. We thought it was funny. It's my stupid name. Who names their child 'Stardust' and expects them to lead a normal life?"

Sara shook her head as she set her tea down. She swiped a hand over her eyes and shook her head. "No, it's okay. I'm okay. It was funny."

Shaking her head, Margaret set her own drink aside and reached out, closing her hand over Sara's. "No, something's upset you. You know we're not laughing at you, right?" She squeezed Sara's hand gently. "It was the whole 'Dusty' thing. Me, the dog, etc." She waved her other hand vaguely. "You know."

Sara tugged her hand free, fighting the rising wave of guilt and shame. She needed to get out of here, get her emotions back under control. Lock everything down again. She couldn't do that with Margaret reaching out, offering comfort she didn't deserve. She looked around for her bag, spotted it on the floor, and reached for it, sliding off the couch as she did so.

"I, um, I've got to go. It's okay, really. I have to get back to the office, get Dusty." She could feel tears welling up again and was desperate to leave before they escaped her rigid control. She was afraid to have Margaret touch her again, afraid that if she did, she might shatter into a million pieces. Before Margaret could say another word, she bolted for the door.

CHAPTER TWELVE

"Damn it!" Margaret threw some bills on the table and sprinted after Sara, heedless of the looks of some of the afternoon regulars. She got to the busy street in time to see Sara disappear around the corner on Pike, heading to First. Margaret sprinted after her and raced around the corner, only to skid to a halt when she spotted Sara doubled over a trash bin, being violently ill.

Margaret stepped beside her and laid a gentle hand on her back, rubbing slowly. "Shh, Sara. It's me. It's okay." She fished in her bag with her other hand, pulling out a wad of wrinkled tissue, and waited for Sara to finish. When she did, Margaret reached down and handed her the tissue. "Here, wipe your mouth. Come on, that's right. Let's go over here."

She guided them both to a bench set against a small storefront, then squatted down in front of Sara. "Will you be okay here, for a minute?" She waited for Sara's nod. "I'm going to pop in there and get you some water. Be right back." She put a hand on Sara's shoulder and gave it a quick squeeze. "Please wait, okay?"

Sara nodded, her eyes far away, as Margaret dashed inside, grabbed the nearest cold water she could find, snapped up a packet of tissue, threw the shopkeeper a ten, and dashed back out again. Sara hadn't moved a muscle, it seemed. Sitting down next to her, Margaret uncapped the water and handed it to her. "Here, rinse. You'll feel better. Promise." Again, Sara just nodded and did as Margaret asked.

They sat in silence for several minutes, buses, cars, people, and bicycles passing at various speeds, all of it a blur to Margaret. Her only thoughts were of the woman beside her. Whatever it was that the misunderstanding with her mom on the farm had triggered in Sara, it was serious, and Margaret hoped she could help. After a while she felt Sara give a slight shiver next to her. "Cold?" When Sara nodded, Margaret rose and offered a hand. "Feel up to walking a bit?" When Sara nodded again, Margaret, keeping her hand around Sara's, led them back around the corner and down toward the water. Sara needed someplace quiet; it was impossible to pull yourself together on a busy street corner.

She had the perfect place in mind.

* * *

Sara let herself be led, trusting Margaret to keep her safe. She felt like crap. Everything she had kept locked up for so long had come thundering back until she couldn't keep it inside anymore. Thankfully she had made it to the trash can in time. She was peripherally aware of the direction they were going and was happy when Margaret steered them past the entrance to Storyville and left, farther down the waterfront. When she saw the sign for Waterfront Park, she relaxed even more. Sure. She could sit in a park for a bit. Get herself together enough to get Dusty, go home, and cry some more. Even if the park wasn't really a "park," but more like a boardwalk.

She was confused, however, when Margaret didn't turn into the park, but instead walked toward the Aquarium, then, dodging them slightly to the left, led her around a partially fenced walkway and out along the long length of the old wharf-turned-attraction. When they reached the end of the building and turned the corner, Sara saw why. Tucked against the back of the aquarium building was an old wooden bench, its arms worn and scarred, its seat dipped and rubbed smooth with age and time. A small brass plaque was embedded into the top rail of the backrest, but Sara couldn't quite make out the words. It didn't matter, really. What mattered was this tiny little oasis in the middle of the craziness of her day.

Of her mind.

With an appreciative sigh, she settled onto the bench and tipped her head back, letting the warmth of the afternoon sun seep into her, warming her down to her bones. Seagulls danced on the wind, crying and complaining about their lack of food as the water lapped against the mollusk-encrusted piers that upheld their isolated space. Ferry horns blew, people laughed and talked, car horns honked, but it all felt far away right now, and for that, Sara was grateful.

"Better?" Margaret's quiet question cut through her swirling thoughts.

"Yes, thanks." Sara rolled her head sideways, feeling the roughened wood of the aquarium wall, and caught Margaret's concerned gaze. "I'm sorry, Margaret. I'm not normally such a drama queen."

"I kind of figured that."

"It's just that," Sara swallowed hard, "just that, this afternoon, the thing with your mom. It got to me."

"Why?" Margaret, too, leaned back into the bench, stretching her legs out before her.

It made it easier, Sara realized, to talk. If Margaret were looking out at the water, she wouldn't be looking at Sara. Wouldn't see inside. Wouldn't know…

"About nine months ago, someone I was close to had a stroke. I was there when it happened."

"I'm sorry."

Again, Margaret's hand reached for hers, and this time Sara didn't pull away. She took the comfort offered, closing her eyes for a moment. She could leave it there, she knew, just let Margaret believe that she had been upset by that memory. She could do that.

It wasn't *lying*, exactly. It was more like…just leaving stuff out.

Coward, her inner voice sneered.

"Did your friend…I mean, was your friend okay?"

Blowing out a long, slow breath, Sara thought about how to answer. Finally, she said, "Yes and no." The silence stretched between them until she felt the tensions would snap her in two, and she realized Margaret was simply going to wait her out. "She is alive, yes. She is, was when I last saw her, I mean, recovering. She'll never be the same person, of course."

"I hear it can really change you." Again, the soft comment offered no censure, no opinion. But why should it? She didn't know, not everything.

And suddenly, Sara wanted it all out there. Wanted to get it over with. When Margaret heard, when she realized who Sara really was, she would be gone. Just do it.

"I left her," she said quietly. "I just…left her."

She waited for Margaret to say something, anything. After another stretch of silence, Margaret turned to her, an eyebrow raised in question. "Okay," she said quietly. "That must have been hard."

Sara blinked. "'That must have been hard,'" she repeated slowly. "That's what you have to say?"

Margaret blinked, clearly surprised by the anger in Sara's voice. "Sure. It would be hard to leave someone you…care for… when they're hurting."

"You don't get it, do you? She had a stroke, and I bailed. Couldn't handle it." She waved a hand wildly. "Ran at the first chance I got." The bile rose in her throat again. She was disgusted by her own inability to stick it out, to stay, when things got rough.

Nodding, Margaret sat forward, her elbows on her knees. "I see. So, your…girlfriend? Okay, girlfriend. She had a stroke and you left."

"No, no. We went to the hospital, two of them. Then were airlifted to another."

"So, you left when she got to the hospital."

"No!" Sara jumped to her feet and paced up and down the short end of the pier, sending seagulls angrily screaming into the sky. "She was in their ICU for days, weeks. They did surgery. Twice. Then rehab in the hospital. Then again at a local rehab place."

As she paced back toward the bench, Sara saw Margaret's brow furrow in puzzlement. *Stop dancing around it, coward. Just tell her.*

"Okay. So. You get your girl to a hospital or three, are there through surgeries, rehab, and then home?" When Sara nodded, she continued. "And once home you decided you had had enough?"

"No." Sara heard her voice catch, felt her throat close again, and bit back another bout of tears. Wiping her eyes, she sank back onto the bench, tucking her feet up and wrapping her arms around her knees. "No. Dev, Devery, she…I came home. She had been home from the rehab place for about two months, and I came home one day and she…she told me to leave. That we were done." She looked up and gave Margaret a wan smile, then shrugged. "So…I did. I left."

Margaret slowly nodded, her eyes never leaving Sara's. She didn't reach out, didn't offer to comfort, just watched her, and Sara felt as if Margaret was looking deep into her soul. Would she see what Sara saw? The coward who bolts the first time she can?

Finally, her eyes still on Sara's, Margaret reached out and touched her cheek, just once. "I'm sorry," she said again. "I cannot imagine how hard this past year has been for you."

Sara shook her head. "For me? I'm not the one who'll never be the same. Who cannot walk without sticks, who can't think past the next step."

"No, but you're the one who was there for it. Watching as they helped her, revived her, taught her to walk again, to eat again, all of it. Your life was upended as much as hers, you know."

"I just feel so…weak, you know? I wanted to leave, so many times! But I stayed. I stayed because she's Dev. We were okay together. And it seemed awful to not stay. But the first time she told me to go, I did! She even gave me the old, 'it's not you, it's me,' line, you know? Giving me 'permission' to bail. However you frame it, I bailed."

"You didn't, you know, but I don't know how to convince you otherwise." Margaret shrugged her shoulders and lifted her hands.

"Remember when you met me on the rooftop of CoGS? That day you came to intimidate me about my bid for the Pine Street building?"

Margaret followed the abrupt topic change with a curious look but protested, "Intimidate? I did *not*."

"You did. But that's beside the point. Remember the woman who was there when you arrived?"

"Yes. If I recall, there was hugging." Margaret's tone was dry, careful.

"Kelly. Another ex. My *only* other ex, actually. I don't get out much. Anyway, she was there to tell me she was getting married."

Margaret's face relaxed, just a bit, but enough that Sara noticed it. "Oh. Well, good for her."

"Yes," Sara said with a biting edge to her agreement. "Bully for Kelly. That's not my point. My point is, after a while if enough people say to you, 'It's not you, it's me,' you begin to wonder if maybe it really IS you after all?"

CHAPTER THIRTEEN

Margaret stared out of her office window at her city view. She liked seeing all the office buildings, imagining behind their blank-faced glass the hundreds of workers, sitting at their desks, scurrying to and from meetings, strolling to copiers, generally being productive. Every bank, insurance company, and developer added to the city's tax base, the improvements to her city. Tax base meant schools and bridges, better highways, community centers, public libraries—everything a world-class city deserved. Margaret was so proud, so honored to be even a small part of that.

After a few minutes, Margaret's thoughts skittered off to Sara. This was becoming an annoying and troubling common occurrence. Their time together this afternoon had served only to add more fuel to that fire. How could she believe she had let anyone down by leaving when asked? Margaret couldn't imagine the amount of stress and anxiety that Sara had been through with Devery's stroke. The uncertainty, the tension. She imagined that Devery asking Sara to leave might have been a defense mechanism or something like that. Whatever the reason, asking Sara to leave had brought her here, to Seattle, and into Margaret's life.

What was it about her that kept Margaret's thoughts returning to her?

Okay, yes, Sara was cute. Not classically beautiful, maybe, but she had great hair and lovely curves, and a casual style that Margaret found...relaxing. Despite the ongoing contention over CoGS, Margaret enjoyed her time with Sara.

She still didn't understand why. She always had thought she needed someone like herself, determined and ambitious. Sara seemed very different, much more willing to act impulsively.

Really, who just picks up a dog off the street?

She could get back to work, but she glanced at her phone lying (plugged in, of course) on her desktop. On an impulse, she picked it up and scrolled down to find Sara's contact info. Margaret shook her head. *The woman doesn't have a phone but she has Messenger. Go figure.*

WinterSM : Wondering how you are after earlier. You okay? Busy?
SaraBellum: Busyish. Working on a grant proposal.
WinterSM: How was the dog?
SaraBellum: Great. My admin is in love with her and was quite happy to Dusty-sit while I had my meltdown.
WinterSM: I wouldn't call it a meltdown. More like a geyser. You needed the release.

Okay, Margaret thought. *That probably falls under the heading of "things that sound better in your head than said out loud."*

SaraBellum: Meltdown, explosion. Whatever. Thanks for listening today. Have I ever mentioned how much I hate paperwork!
WinterSM: Really? I like it. I love getting it off my desk, I feel like I've accomplished something.

SaraBellum: Maybe you would like to come on over and do this proposal for me, then.
WinterSM: No, thanks. Let me guess what you would rather be doing.
SaraBellum: Bet you get it in one try.
WinterWinterSM: It involves putting your fingers in dirt, right?
SaraBellum: See, I knew you would get it! Yes, I would always rather be in the garden. What about you?

Margaret was puzzled. Was Sara asking about her notoriously black thumb? Margaret could destroy any houseplant in ten days flat.

WinterSM: What do you mean? I don't garden.
SaraBellum: No, silly, I meant your secret hobby. A guilty pleasure.

There was truly only one thing that qualified. This meant exposing herself a bit more to Sara, but somehow it seemed to be the right thing to do. Margaret took a deep breath, released it and began to type.

WinterSM: Don't tell anyone. Especially my mother.
SaraBellum: Yes?
WinterSM: I read romance novels. The trashier, the better.

There was a long pause as Margaret watched the blinking dots for Sara's reply. Was she staring at the phone in shock? Doubled over at her desk in helpless laughter? Showing it to all her coworkers?

SaraBellum: I would not have guessed that.
WinterSM: It's embarrassing. And it's not just lesbian romance. Mainstream, too.
SaraBellum: I would say surprising but not embarrassing. I like you better for knowing it.

Margaret stared at that for a bit. She had to remember that she was still in a competitive bid situation with the woman. She didn't want Sara to think she was softhearted or sentimental.

WinterSM: Not only that, but I really don't like goat cheese. Especially my mother's goat cheese.

Enough true confessions, she thought. *Time to turn the conversation.* She had only messaged her in the first place because the link was at the bottom of Sara's email and the play on words for her screen name had made her smile.

WinterSM: OK, your turn. I told you some of my deepest, darkest secrets. Now you.

Margaret hit enter and wondered if Sara would bite.

SaraBellum: I don't think so. Besides, what's the big deal about not liking your mother's homemade cheese?

Margaret shuddered. She couldn't believe she shared that. If she hadn't just been nearly force-fed homemade pizza covered liberally with her mom's newest "artisan" creation...

WinterSM: You don't know my mom. Okay, you've met her, but...Anyway, come on. I dare you.

She hit "send" and sat back, smirking as she popped over to her email. She was sure Sara Chandler had a wild side that was a mile wide. The cutoff denim shorts she had been wearing when they had met had spoken volumes. She's probably trying to pick something tame to share, she thought. *Might be a while.* Before she got through the next email in her inbox, however, the soft chime of an incoming text pulled her back.

SaraBellum: Fine. I don't really have any...Oh. Sometimes, when I'm really stressed about something, I'll sing like a virgin in the shower.

Huh? Margaret's mouth dropped open. How does someone sing like a virgin? Her fingers worked faster than her brain and she hit "send" before realizing she had actually typed that question out.

WinterSM: How do you sing like a virgin?

The three dots that signaled someone was typing rippled for a long moment while Margaret puzzled over the question. The dots disappeared, then reappeared again. Then maddeningly, they disappeared again. Realizing she was staring at a screen waiting for a text to pop up, Margaret clicked back into the document she was working on and began typing. The message, when it popped up, momentarily confused her.

SaraBellum: I assume like anyone else would.
WinterSM: Um...do virgins sing differently? Or just when in the shower?

She hit "send" again and leaned back, her throat suddenly very dry. Their chat had taken a turn she had never expected. She read Sara's comment again and her eyes widened again. She quickly began typing before her brain could remind her of this afternoon's conversation.

WinterSM: No. Wait. You cannot be telling me that you're...

Before she could finish a new message popped up.

SaraBellum: You're kidding, right?

Quickly erasing what she had been about to ask, Margaret answered carefully.

WinterSM: About what? Aren't you the one talking about singing virgins?

This time the pause was longer and the rippling dots that signaled Sara's typing seemed to simply taunt Margaret. The dots disappeared, then returned before disappearing again, and this time Margaret growled at the screen in frustration and determinedly stayed there. This response she *would* wait for. Finally a new text popped up.

SaraBellum: You've never heard like a virgin?

First singing and now hearing? Honestly.

WinterSM: OK, clearly I'm missing something. How does someone sing like a virgin, let alone hear like one?

The wait for a response was so long this time that Margaret opened a browser window and pondered how to go about searching for "sing like a virgin" without getting ten billion seedy responses. When her chat window chimed, she switched back to look. Another message balloon popped up with arrows pointing to the link above it and a challenge.

SaraBellum: Click me. I dare you.

One click and suddenly in the tiny chat window was a YouTube video link featuring the sultry gaze of the 1980s big-haired Madonna, tight tank top, multiple necklaces swinging as she wandered through the streets of Venice belting out boppy lyrics with…was that a lion?

Margaret's rich, warm laughter rolled through the empty office as the name of the song registered. That's why she liked Sara. She was so different. Funny. Unusual, unique, even.

Margaret was sure she would be bored with Sara eventually. This kind of frivolity couldn't be sustained in a relationship of any kind. After a while, it would become cloying, maybe even annoying.

She clicked on the link again.

* * *

Energized by the exchange with Sara, Margaret double-checked her task list for the day, electronically checking off items as she read. She was left with one task that she'd assigned to Jeremy that morning, and she decided to take a stroll and assure herself the delivery had been made.

She walked out to the open area filled with cubicles. Before she got to Jeremy's desk, she saw the intern—Daisy, right?—sitting in her desk chair, staring vacantly at her desktop.

Margaret stopped abruptly. What was going on?

Sometime that afternoon it had started raining, something that was hardly surprising. Daisy's curly hair was as damp as if someone had dumped a large cup of water on her head. Whatever fasteners she had used that morning had failed to contain her unruly curls, and half of her hairdo was in her face. Her suit was soaked across the shoulders and damp halfway down her sleeves.

"Daisy?" Margaret said.

The young woman looked up with hollow eyes, mascara smeared below them making her look like an aging raccoon.

"Are you all right?" Margaret asked.

She did not respond as expected. Daisy looked away from Margaret and burst into tears—not just a tear or two, but great, loud, chest-heaving sobs. She sprang up from her desk, shoving the desk chair away so hard it bounced into the padded wall of the cubicle.

She ran toward the ladies' room, zigzagging through other employees. She was limping badly. Had she injured herself? After a moment Margaret realized that Daisy's gait was lopsided because she was wearing one high heel and one shoe that no longer had a heel attached to it.

What in heaven's name had happened?

Jeremy appeared at her elbow.

"What did you say to her?" he demanded.

Margaret turned on him, eyes narrowing.

"I'm sorry?" She used her frostiest voice.

"Sorry, Ms. Winters," he apologized quickly. "She's just had a rough day is all."

"Well, I figured that out for myself," Margaret said dryly. Unlike her mother, Jeremy caught the tone of voice. His Adam's apple bobbed up and down a couple of times.

"I just came by to make sure you delivered the mylars for the Northgate project," Margaret said.

Now the goatee started to shake. *Uh-oh*, Margaret thought.

"My office," she said. "Right now."

Jeremy settled into her visitor's chair, shifting uncomfortably as if he couldn't find a good position.

Margaret said, "I'm going to take a wild guess. You didn't deliver the mylars, did you?"

He shook his head. The mylars were big, plastic-coated copies of the final development plans, in this case for a new mixed-use development in Northgate, consisting of both residential and commercial uses. The final versions had to be signed off on by both the developers and the Planning Commission before they could be filed. It was a straightforward task but essential to the process.

"You sent Daisy, right?" Margaret continued.

He nodded, looking even more miserable than before.

"I'm still working on the research on the Stockton Family Trust and I thought she might want to get out and..."

Margaret lifted a hand to stop the flow of words.

"All right," she said. "I see. So you'd better tell me what happened."

"I had her put the mylars in one of the big mailing tubes from the mail room. I thought it would protect them, since it looked like it might rain. Anyway, I got her off to the light rail with directions to the developer's office."

He sighed, his goatee starting to wobble again.

Margaret sat back in her chair. Her curiosity was on overload. What could possibly have gone wrong?

Jeremy finally said, "I guess she got distracted or something. Anyway she missed her stop."

"Where did she end up?"

"Er. Um. Actually, Angle Lake."

The only word that described Margaret's feeling was dumbfounded.

"Angle Lake," she repeated. "That's at the other end of town. The end of the light rail line. In the opposite direction from Northgate."

"Um. Yes, that's right."

"She got on the light rail going the wrong way." Margaret was still stunned.

"Uh-huh."

"Okay. What happened then?"

"She called me. Once I figured out where she'd gone wrong, I told her exactly where to go to get back on the light rail. So she got on the train going the right direction this time."

"She couldn't go any other direction," Margaret pointed out.

"Well. Yes. So, anyway she got back on the train."

"And went to Northgate?"

"Well. No. She got lost again, got off the train too early, I think. Anyway, she tried to call me again, but I was in a planning meeting and didn't get the call. So as she was getting off the train, she broke her heel and couldn't really walk very far. She got some coffee and tried to look at a light rail map and on Google to figure out how to get to Northgate. And finally she got back on the train."

"And did she manage to get lost a third time?" Margaret asked.

"No, this time she made it to the developer's office." He hesitated.

"And?"

"She didn't have the mylars," Jeremy admitted.

"She what!"

He sighed once again.

"She left them on the train."

"Oh, please tell me they're not traveling around somewhere by themselves on the light rail system."

He shook his head.

"She somehow managed to get a cab and track down the car. Unfortunately, when she got there…"

"I'm afraid to ask."

"Well, the police were there. They were waiting for the bomb squad."

"The bomb squad?"

"You know how things are these days," Jeremy said rapidly. "Everyone is so bomb conscious. You can't leave a package at the airport, or in a public place anywhere, or…"

"I get it."

"Somebody decided the mylars looked like a giant pipe bomb, I guess. There was no label on the mailing tube. When Daisy showed up and said it was hers, they, um, detained her. They got a bomb-sniffing dog in and then one of those portable x-ray machines."

Margaret could picture the scene. How could one person screw up so many times on one simple errand? Jeremy must be sleeping with her, Margaret was certain. There was no way he would put up with this Mariana Trench-depth of incompetence for any other reason.

"Anyway," Jeremy continued, "by the time the cops finally cut her loose and she got back to the developer's office, he'd already left for another meeting. She called me. She was pretty hysterical at that point."

"I would imagine so."

"I left and drove up to get her," Jeremy said. "We tracked him down and waited until he got out and got him to sign the mylars."

"So they're back safely?" Margaret had been having serious doubts as the story proceeded.

"Back in the file room," Jeremy said. "The Planning Commission has a study session in the morning and the chair will sign them then."

Margaret tapped her fingers on her desktop. Jeremy was sitting stiffly now, clearly preparing himself for whatever was going to happen next, yelling or throwing things or perhaps getting fired.

Margaret had no intention of firing him, of course, but something had to happen. He looked so nervous that Margaret decided she should make him wait for whatever she was going to do. A written reprimand ought to be enough, she determined. It would stay in his personnel file and that would be punishment enough for an ambitious man like him.

Daisy was another problem altogether. Jeremy was in charge of the internship program and Margaret was loathe to fire Daisy out from under him. Perhaps there was another solution.

"We'll discuss this in the morning," she decided. "My office, nine o'clock. Don't be late. And be prepared to discuss what you propose to do about Daisy. Is that clear?"

As she had hoped, this declaration made him look even more miserable. Now that the mylars were safe, she couldn't have hoped for a better result.

CHAPTER FOURTEEN

"Jeremy, where are the plats for the Ocean View mall project?"

Margaret could always summon him to her office, of course, but sometimes she liked surprising him at his own. For one thing, she got to stand over him, which gave her a psychological advantage if nothing else. Especially when she had yet more evidence of another instance of sloppy work.

"They're not in the file room?"

Margaret bestowed upon him her best withering look. "If the plats were properly filed, I wouldn't be asking you for them, would I? Weren't you the one who took them out? No one else is working on them, as far as I know. I need to double-check the sign square footage requirements."

"I can do that for you," he answered quickly.

Margaret sighed. "I know you can. But it will be really difficult to do without the plats. Which, as you know, are very large and unlikely to have accidently fallen into your coffee cup. So will you get them from wherever they might be and bring them to my office?"

His eyes darted around and Margaret wondered if he thought the documents might suddenly pop up across the room. "Of course, Ms. Winters. Right away."

"And while I'm here, how are we coming on the alternative CoGS site project?"

He seemed to relax slightly at the change of subject.

"We've identified three other locations. Daisy and I are working on a PowerPoint presentation with photos, specifications, maps, as much detail as we can. I thought you might want to present it to the board."

Margaret considered. Maybe. But the person she needed to persuade was Sara—the way to win this property was to get her to withdraw the CoGS bid, because Margaret was convinced she would never win in a fair fight. Family, after all.

She hadn't been entirely pleased with Jeremy's decision to keep Daisy on, but he had agreed to restrict her duties to research—in the office, where he could keep an eye on her. Still, as long as she didn't foul up again, she didn't suppose it mattered.

Margaret's thoughts shifted to Sara as she walked back to her office. Why exactly was she seeing Sara? She certainly wanted Sara to withdraw the CoGS bid, but she didn't feel like she was being deliberately manipulative. Or was she? Maybe she didn't understand her own motives.

No. She actually sort of liked Sara. Okay, more than sort of, which was more than a little surprising. Sara seemed caring, calm, smart but not pretentious, but there was nothing about her that was Margaret's usual cup of tea. She wasn't ambitious in any way Margaret recognized and seemed to care about things Margaret never gave much thought to—like vegetables. And plastic straws. And stray dogs.

Sara really was, in fact, a lot like Margaret's mother, and this growing realization made her ever so slightly queasy.

* * *

"You have a nice office," Sara said, looking out over the view of the city from Margaret's window. "It's about three times the size of mine."

"Well, you spend a lot of time outdoors, right?" Margaret placed the takeout bowls on her conference table with glasses of water. "That's your real office."

Sara smiled. "You are right. The office is just for paperwork. Which I hate, by the way."

"You may have mentioned that." At Sara's confused look, Margaret tipped her head toward her phone. "Chat, yesterday." She sat down and placed her paper napkin carefully in her lap before popping open the lid on her salad. "I'm good at paperwork. You can't succeed in government work without it."

"I'm sure a truer statement has never been made. So, what's for lunch?"

"You told me to surprise you. I have a niçoise salad. Yours is toasted quinoa and salmon. I'm happy to swap if you would rather."

Sara stopped with her fork hovering over her meal. "Salmon?"

Margaret grinned at her. "Responsibly sourced wild sockeye. I checked."

Sara returned the smile and said, "I may convert you yet."

If my mother hasn't managed it in thirty-seven years, I doubt you're going to accomplish it in a couple of weeks.

Sara munched happily. "This is good. Do you usually eat at your desk?"

The question surprised Margaret. She nodded. "Unless I have a lunch meeting, which I probably have a couple of times a week. They can be challenging if it's an event of some kind, neighborhood associations, community organizations, like that. They tend to default to overcooked meat, limp pasta, and soggy vegetables. Blech."

"Golly, you make it sound delicious."

"If that sounds good, wait until you taste my cooking."

"You cook?"

"Not even a little bit. I have a handsome collection of takeout menus from every restaurant in the city that will give me one. It's an impressive sight. And I have a favorite bakery right down the block from my condo. So all of my needs are met."

"Well, for food, at least," Sara said.

Margaret nearly choked on a piece of tuna and groped for her water glass.

"Are you all right?"

"Fine. Wrong pipe. Reminding myself—esophagus, not trachea."

"Good reminder."

Was Sara flirting with her? She certainly hoped so.

They ate in companionable silence for a while. When Sara pushed her dish away, she propped her chin in her hand and gazed directly at Margaret.

"Why did you invite me all the way down here for lunch?" she asked.

Always so direct.

"It wasn't to see your office, I'm guessing," she continued.

Margaret sighed. She had been of two minds about the invitation, but she wanted the business part of the meeting on her own turf, to keep it professional. The problem was her lack of professional feelings where Sara was concerned.

Well, actually the problem was all those other feelings where Sara was concerned.

Deep breath. You can do this. Remember what's at stake.

Margaret folded her hands on the table. "Look, I know we agreed not to talk about the Stockton Industries building while we're, um…"

"Dating?" Sara suggested disingenuously.

"Er, yes. Seeing each other. But we've done a lot of work to try to, ah, help. CoGS, I mean."

"How so?"

Margaret leaned forward. This was the moment. It was time to bring all her logic to bear.

"The Stockton building is the only place we can use to close the Pacific Rim deal. It's so important to the city, I feel as if

I have to do everything I can to get it, but I understand how important the garden is to you. So, we found you options."

"Options? You mean alternative sites?"

Margaret sat back happily. "Exactly."

Sara shook her head.

"Margaret, don't you think we looked at lots of possibilities before we went with Stockton Industries? I must have considered every abandoned warehouse, empty parking area, and vacant lot in the city."

She hadn't counted on that. She had assumed that CoGS had picked the building because Sara was a family member.

"I don't know what you looked at, but we have three really good options for you. I've got a PowerPoint for you here."

Sara was quiet for a minute.

"I'll look at it," she said at last. "As a favor to you. It will take a lot of convincing. No promises."

Margaret enjoyed few things more than a presentation, even to an audience of one. She had to admit that Jeremy had done a good job of assembling the pitch: quality photos of the sites, facts and figures neatly presented, even a list of pros and cons for each location. Sara sat quietly during the entire demonstration, no questions or comments. Margaret found it a little unnerving but pushed through.

The silence after she finished was deafening.

"Well?" Margaret said. "What do you think? I think my first choice might be the South King Street…"

"Margaret. We looked at King Street. We looked at the Alaskan Way site too."

"They're both great alternatives," Margaret said with as much enthusiasm as she could manage.

Sara heaved a great sigh.

"Neither will work. Remember the point of a community garden is to address the food desert issue. Both of these sites are too remote."

"King Street is only a few miles, on the bus line."

"Margaret. The people we're talking about work, every day some of them, busing tables or cleaning office toilets. They have to take public transportation everywhere, which costs them time and energy and money. They have to be able to walk to a community garden for it to help them. Those two locations are just too far away from the people who need to use the garden."

Margaret felt her grip on the situation slipping away.

"And the Masters location?"

Sara shook her head.

"I hadn't seen that one before. But location isn't the problem there. It's size. The usable garden area is only a little over twenty-five hundred square feet and that's not close to enough land. We're looking to have at least fifty families put in gardens."

How could this not have worked? Why wasn't she listening? What on earth was she going to do?

Sara reached across the table and took Margaret's hand. Margaret reacted as she always did when Sara touched her, with a warm tingle that seemed to shimmer through her body. She had never felt this before and she knew it was special. But why, oh why, did it have to be stubborn Granola Girl?

"Margaret, I know you and your staff went to a lot of trouble to put this together. And I appreciate it, I really do, both the idea and the effort. But this garden matters to me, just as the Pacific Rim deal matters to you."

"I don't see…they're not even close to comparable…I mean…"

Why did Sara keep making her stutter? *Drat!*

"Margaret," Sara repeated in her calmest voice. "We are going to have to drop this. Unless this is a deal breaker for you."

"A deal breaker?"

"If you want to stop seeing me because of this, I understand."

Stop seeing her? It hadn't occurred to Margaret. Should she? How could she date Sara if she lost the Pacific Rim deal?

How could she not? No one had ever made her feel this way.

Sara withdrew her hand and Margaret missed her touch.

"Good," Sara said. "Because I don't want it to be a deal breaker. In fact, now that I've seen your office, I think it's time I see your condo. Are you free for dinner on Friday? I'll arrange a visit for Dusty with Mom and Dad."

"You are not," Margaret said, "expecting me to cook, I assume."

"No, I want to see your expertise at manipulating all those gourmet menus. I'll bring wine, how about that?"

The flutter grew in Margaret's stomach. This was sounding a lot like a sleepover date, and she was equal parts excited and terrified.

Sara looked as if she were feeling something else. It took Margaret a moment to identify it.

Sara looked supremely happy.

CHAPTER FIFTEEN

Margaret poured the last of the wine, equally dividing it between their two glasses.

"Good choice on the Syrah," she said. "Yakima Valley, you said?"

Sara sipped delicately.

"Yes. Red Willow Vineyards. It's one of my favorites. It also went great with the kabobs."

"I do love grilled food," Margaret said. The later the evening got, the more she found herself resorting to small talk. Which was silly. It wasn't like she had never had a woman overnight before.

But this felt different. Because Sara was different, and Margaret knew it. By unspoken agreement, neither Stockton Industries nor Pacific Rim were mentioned. She had expected it to hang over them, but she found they had so much more to talk about.

Sara toyed with the stem of her wineglass. "Tell me about your last girlfriend."

"Why?"

Sara laughed. "Because I asked, maybe? No ulterior motive. Just curious."

"Bobbi was her name. She was a corporate exec in a big real estate company. We dated pretty seriously for three years or so."

"What did you like about her?" Sara asked.

That surprised Margaret. Usually people asked why they broke up.

"She was successful," Margaret said. "Ambitious, hard worker, seemed to care for the same things I did."

"Seemed to?"

Margaret drank some more wine, trying to decide what to say.

Finally she said, "In the end, money was all that really mattered to her. She measured everything by how much people made or how much they spent or how much things cost. She was always worried about her next raise or bonus—or mine. I mean, it's not that money doesn't matter. It's not just the only measure of success."

"No, it's not," Sara agreed. "Though I concede that it's easy for someone like me to say that. That's why I try to remember how few people are as privileged as I am."

Margaret got a warm glow in her belly. *Must be the wine.*

"I like that about you," Margaret admitted. "Whatever we may disagree on, I know your motives are always good ones, I do."

"And I know," Sara said quietly, "that you are doing what you think is the right thing. And now that we've settled that, I think it's time for another activity."

"Um, jigsaw puzzle? Gin rummy? Binge watching *House Hunters*?"

"Nope."

Sara slid across the couch and leaned into Margaret.

"This."

She put her hands on either side of Margaret's face to hold her gently. This was a real kiss, all the softness and flavor and desire Margaret could have hoped for. When Sara broke away, Margaret murmured, "Oh, wow."

"Wow is good, yes?"

"Wow is…wow."

"More?"

"Oh, yeah."

Margaret was liking this Sara very, very much. She might be all soft curves and Granola Girl Zen, but apparently she had a clear idea of what she wanted.

Margaret moved her hands down to enjoy the lush velvety skin under Sara's blouse. Stroking the curve from waist to hip seemed to be eliciting a gratifying sound, a bit like that of a purring kitten.

It had been a long while since Margaret had actually made out and she found she was enjoying it. Her body, always a bit slow to warm up, was heating in a very satisfactory way.

She had been fantasizing about Sara's décolletage since she met her, and it was time to enjoy her opportunity. She fumbled with pulling the sweater over Sara's head.

Sara sat up on her knees. She reached down and pulled the sweater off with one smooth motion. Margaret thought it was the sexiest thing she had ever seen, Sara in her black bra, leaning back down into her mouth.

Kissing the soft skin between Sara's breasts was as close to heaven as Margaret expected to get in this life. She couldn't tell which one of them was enjoying it more.

And more was what she wanted. She fumbled around, trying to unhook Sara's bra but couldn't quite manage it around her back.

Sara smiled and said, "Am I going to have to help you with everything?"

Margaret said, "For some reason, my motor skills seem to be going haywire. I think it's your fault."

"I certainly hope so."

Sara got the bra off and Margaret couldn't help the happy moan as she filled her hands with Sara's creamy soft breasts. Nothing had ever felt better.

When she finally released them to fumble for the button on Sara's pants, Sara stopped her with a touch. "Not yet. You need to catch up."

Margaret trembled a little as Sara slowly unbuttoned Margaret's blouse. Three buttons down she saw a flying object in her peripheral vision. "Wait!" she exclaimed.

Sara stopped immediately. "What's wrong? Are you okay? Do you not want me to…"

"No. I mean, button."

"Button?"

"Lost a button, it came off."

"Do we need to worry about this now?"

Margaret swallowed. "It's…they're pearl. We'll have trouble finding it on the white rug and they were from my grandmother and…"

"Margaret. Margaret. Calm down. We'll find it."

It took a solid five minutes of patting and groping the rug—not each other—to find the missing button, which had managed to fly several feet away, to near the fireplace. Sara held it up in triumph. "Aha!"

Margaret breathed a long sigh. "Thank you. I know it seems silly, but…"

"Not at all. It's been weeks since I interrupted a make-out session to search for a missing object." She glanced down at herself and added, "Topless, that is."

Margaret slumped back onto the couch. "Oh, Sara, I'm sorry."

"Don't be. We have all night, sweet pea. That is, assuming, you want to finish what we started."

The lush Sara was beautiful, there was no other word for it. "I think we should go to the bedroom now."

"Lead the way."

* * *

Margaret was accustomed to taking the lead in the bedroom, at least in the beginning. As with the rest of her life, setting the pace made her feel secure and in control.

Sara had a different agenda, apparently.

"We are suffering," Sara announced, "from a serious disparity in clothing status. Such as you're still wearing most of yours. I would like to take them off now."

At that moment there was nothing more in the Milky Way galaxy that Margaret wanted. Sara finished unbuttoning the blouse with the fancy buttons very carefully. She laid it aside and took a moment to admire Margaret's lacy red bra.

Sara smiled up at her. "Special outfit just for me?" she asked.

Margaret suppressed a pleasant shudder. "Just for you," she repeated.

"Much as I love it, let's take this off, shall we?"

Margaret found herself enjoying this more and more. She reached behind to unhook the bra and Sara reached up and slid the straps off.

There was always that first moment of uncertainty, since Margaret was self-conscious about not being exactly voluptuous. But Sara smiled and stroked the soft skin above, below, and in between.

"You're lovely," she whispered, and Margaret felt the warmth run through her body.

"Maybe we could move faster?" Margaret said. "I'm getting a little…um…"

Sara gave her a smile that moved beyond warm and sexy to positively, well, smutty. It took Margaret all her self-control not to knock her backward onto the bed.

She shouldn't have worried. In a move that would have impressed a black belt in judo, Sara had Margaret on the bed, on her back, pants at her ankles before she could blink twice. Sara was pressing her warm, smooth flesh against her in many delightful places.

Sara did a slow body rub, up and down. Margaret tried not to grab everything at the same time. She finally settled for her hands on the delightful curvy ass and gave Sara a little squeeze.

Sara gave plenty of attention to all the good bits on the way down Margaret's body. Eventually Margaret released her grip, then released everything and lost herself in Sara's touch.

So, so good. Mouth and hands, soft yummy noises, sometimes almost a purr, everything Sara did heated Margaret up from her core. Sara knew when to slow down and speed up and Margaret was so filled with pleasure she could hardly bear it.

When Sara finally focused on the endgame, Margaret had the best orgasm she could recall, joy and release together. So, so good.

"Oh, my God," Margaret finally muttered.

Sara eased back up to Margaret's shoulder. "I'll take that as a compliment."

"That was the intent."

Margaret reached down and grasped another comfortable handful of Sara. "I think," she said, "we could try some other things now."

Sara's smutty grin returned. "Great idea," she said.

CHAPTER SIXTEEN

Margaret awoke to two overwhelming sensations. The first was the expanse of warm, soft woman cuddled against her back. She could feel Sara's breasts nestled against her back like a satisfying pair of pillows. Sara's legs matched the curve of her own.

They fit perfectly, Margaret's angular frame and curvy Sara, made for each other. Who would have thought it?

The second overwhelming sensation was that she really, really had to pee. The thought of leaving the nice warm nest was torture, but there was no denying the trip had to happen. She eased out as gently as she could. Sara made a noise but seemed to resume sleeping peacefully.

Margaret decided she had time to eliminate her morning breath and scrub off the remnants of last night's makeup. Refreshed and revitalized, she returned to the bedroom to find Sara gone, her pillow still dented from her head.

Where was she? The smell of coffee brewing answered her question.

Margaret grabbed her robe and followed her nose to the kitchen.

"Hi!" Sara greeted her with a full, steaming mug.

Margaret said, "You're wearing my shirt."

"Yes. My clothes never made it out of the living room. So decadent. How's the coffee?"

"Life-saving. Sorry I woke you."

"You didn't. It wasn't any fun in bed without you, that's all. Did you sleep?"

Margaret laughed. "When? You are insatiable, woman."

Sara fanned herself. "Why, thank you, ma'am. I do believe you were a fully participating member of the Cirque de Sex."

"I do believe you are right. Are you hungry?" Margaret was torn between eyeing the lovely cleavage revealed by the too-tight blouse and the expanse of shapely leg exposed beneath the hemline.

She raised her gaze to Sara's eyes. "Steaming" seemed to be a good description of her mood.

"Do you need to finish your coffee?" Sara whispered.

Margaret took one more sip and set the mug down on the counter. "I'm good."

"You certainly are."

This time it was slow and sweet and tender. Sara lay back and let Margaret enjoy her, every nook and cranny. When she came, it was with a cry of happiness that made Margaret weep with happiness.

They fell asleep in bliss.

* * *

Margaret woke for the second time that day. She gave a delicious stretch. Waking up next to Sara was getting to be one of her favorite things. Good thing it was Saturday and they had plenty of time.

Saturday!

"Damn! What time is it?"

Sara stirred. "Whatzit?" she muttered.

"Oh, my God. Sara, wake up! You have to wake up! Mrs. Stein!"

"Huh. What?"

"Mrs. Stein! She'll be here in a few minutes!"

Margaret threw off the covers and scrambled to her closet. Clothes began flying out randomly, landing on the floor. A sweater actually plopped onto Sara's head.

"Margaret! Calm down. Is it your cleaning lady?"

"No!" The answer was muffled. "Oh, my God, the bakery!"

"The baker will be here? Margaret, what baker?"

"Not *baker*, baker-*ee*," she said, emphasizing the second half of the word as she continued to sort through her clothing.

"Okay, I give up," Sara said. "Are you dating Mrs. Stein?"

Margaret's head emerged momentarily.

"My neighbor. Friends. We have tea and cookies every Saturday. I haven't been to the bakery yet and she'll be here in a few minutes, sometimes she's early…"

"Okay." Sara got out of bed and began gathering clothes. "We're fine. You get dressed and go to the bakery. I'll stay here and greet her and we'll chat until you get back." She cocked her head. "I'm assuming she knows you're gay."

"Of course." Margaret was hopping on one leg, trying to fit the other into her jeans.

"Um, Margaret?"

"I don't have time—"

"Those are my jeans."

"Oh." Margaret glared at the jeans as she tugged them off, then found her own and quickly slipped them on.

"So she won't be shocked that you had an overnight guest. We'll be fine. Go get what you need at the bakery."

"Okay. Okay." Margaret was out of breath. "But as liberal as Mrs. Stein is, you should probably be wearing clothes when you let her in."

"Fair enough. I'll work on that."

* * *

When the doorbell rang, Sara was not only dressed but was working on a second cup of tea. When she opened the door, Margaret's neighbor blinked once in surprise but recovered quickly. "Oh, I'm terribly sorry. I'm interrupting."

She turned to leave, but Sara quickly reached out and touched her arm. "No, please, wait. You're Mrs. Stein, yes? Margaret will be right back. She's expecting you. Please come in."

"If you're sure, dear. I don't want to intrude."

Sara shook her head and smiled, closing the door behind them as she steered Margaret's guest into the sunlit kitchen. "You're not interrupting at all. Would you like some tea?"

"Oh, I would love some, thank you."

Sara busied herself with pouring out a second cup, making sure to set out on the glass-topped table the cream and sugar Margaret told her that Mrs. Stein liked. She turned to find the older woman still standing in the kitchen doorway.

"Please sit down. I promise, Margaret will be back soon." She held out a hand. "I'm Sara Chandler."

Mrs. Stein shook her hand and then accepted the teacup as she settled into the padded wooden chair. "Lovely to meet you, Sara." She added cream and sugar to her tea and stirred gently before taking a cautious sip. "Ah, wonderful. Thank you." Helping herself to one of the small cookies Sara had set out, she asked, "So, where did our Margaret run off to? Not work, I hope."

"No, she's down at the bakery." Sara smiled as she recalled the nearly frantic look on Margaret's face as she had dashed out the door.

"So," Mrs. Stein said, taking another long sip of her tea, "have you known Margaret long?"

"Just a few weeks."

"Ah."

She packed a lot into that little word, Sara thought.

"And I'm going to guess you met at work."

Sara cocked her head a little. "Sort of. It's complicated. Good guess, though. How did you know?"

With a sigh, Mrs. Stein grimaced slightly, the move emphasizing the lines of her soft skin. "It's Margaret. All she does is work, poor thing."

"Well, as I said, it's complicated. Technically we met because of a work-related issue, but, in all fairness, our first date was a blind date set up by our moms."

"How charming! And old-fashioned." She paused, then added, "And how unlike Margaret's mother."

"I guess it is at that," Sara responded, surprised by the comment about Carol.

"And you like her?"

Sara had several possible responses to that, but settled for, "I do like her. Very much."

This clearly pleased Mrs. Stein, whose face settled again, smoothing out the concerned creases. "Good. Good. Because she may have told you I'm moving soon, and I didn't like leaving her all alone. She really needs someone to love."

Sara mulled this comment over a moment, taken aback by the comment. *Love? Whoa, there, lady.* Her instinctive reaction was to pull back, to deny that there was anything like that at all, between them. She bent her head and picked at a roughened edge of her thumbnail while Mrs. Stein placidly sipped her tea in the quiet kitchen. The ticking of the clock on the wall sounded very loud all of a sudden, filling the silence left by Mrs. Stein's words.

"...*someone to love*..." echoed through her brain. She wouldn't have slept with Margaret and certainly wouldn't have stayed the whole night if she didn't *care* for her, but... Glancing up, she saw Mrs. Stein studying her intently. She lifted a shoulder and took another sip of her tea before saying, finally, "Don't we all need somebody to love?"

Mrs. Stein nodded vigorously. "Certainly. But it's especially important in her case."

Sara was becoming more intrigued with the conversation. She leaned forward and planted her elbow on the table, her chin on her open palm. "Why is that?"

"She never had much of a home growing up. Not that she's said as much, mind, it's more of what she *hasn't* said. Her mother was always pillar to post and I don't think Margaret learned a lot about families or stable relationships. And then there was that *commune*," Mrs. Stein's lips tightened, as if she were holding words back, before adding, "No real home, or family, really. She desperately wants one, you know."

Sara eased back again, fighting the urge to deny, to protest. Jesus, they had had *one* night together and Margaret's sweet old neighbor was practically picking out baby names! "Um, that's not immediately...obvious."

"You're right. She hides it well." Mrs. Stein glanced around and then leaned conspiratorially across the table, her voice unnecessarily low. "If I tell you something, can you keep the secret from Margaret?"

Sara blinked in surprise as she, too, reflexively glanced around before chiding herself for the move. *Honestly, who could possibly overhear us?* Margaret hadn't said anything about her neighbor being unstable, but here she was, suddenly wanting to share secrets with a perfect stranger. Playing along, Sara nodded. "Sure, okay."

Her eyes bright with humor and her secret, Mrs. Stein settled back again, wrapping her hands around her teacup. "The first time I went out with my Georgie, he was poorer than a church mouse. But when he came to pick me up, he had a fistful of daisies clutched tightly, hidden behind his back. I'm sure they were the cheapest he could find. But he bought them for me. And to spiff himself up, he had gotten a red and white striped carnation for his jacket lapel. It was the sweetest thing." Her gaze left Sara's and wandered out of the window into the cloudless sky. "He was so dashing, so handsome, my Georgie."

"Aw, that's so sweet." Not at all clear on where this was heading, Sara watched Mrs. Stein as she blinked her eyes rapidly, then took another sip of her tea.

"Yes, yes he was. Anyway," she said, returning her gaze to Sara. "Every Friday, without fail, since about a week after I told

Margaret that story, I find a bunch of daisies with a red and white striped carnation tucked in the middle of them, resting in a long white box, right outside my door. No card, no note, just a lovely box of flowers."

"And you're sure they're from Margaret?" Sara tried to picture Margaret picking up a big white box of flowers every Friday and sneaking down the hall to deliver them to her neighbor. Yes, she was discovering that Margaret had a softer side, was not nearly as hard-edged as she had seemed when they first met. But she didn't really strike Sara as the sneaky flower-delivering type.

"Well..." Mrs. Stein set her half-eaten cookie delicately on the plate and brushed crumbs from her fingers, clearly disappointed in Sara's lack of reaction. "One afternoon I was getting ready to meet Anna O'Grady from the seventh floor for our weekly dinner and I realized I had left my handbag on my key table. So I popped back up for it, and as I came around the corner I saw Margaret laying the box at my doorstep. She was being so careful and quiet that I waited until she was inside her own apartment before I came down the hallway to retrieve my handbag."

"Oh. Wow." Sara leaned back. "So, how long has she been doing this?" Sara felt she had lost some points with Margaret's neighbor for doubting her—and by extension, Margaret—and suddenly, it was important to her that Mrs. Stein liked her. Unwilling to identify why, she instead refilled Mrs. Stein's tea and slid the plate of cookies closer to her. "And, wait. Why is it a secret?"

"Well, my dear," Mrs. Stein nodded her thanks for the tea, "she's been delivering those flowers for nearly two years, now. She doesn't know that I know, and I want her to think I am completely fooled."

"Why?" Sara asked.

Mrs. Stein smiled a knowing smile. "As I mentioned earlier," she said. "Her mother is a bit of a...free spirit."

Sara grinned. "I've met her."

"Ah. Well, then. You would understand. I think Margaret never really felt valued or successful. She's certainly making up for that in her career now. But deep inside, I believe she is, at heart, a romantic, sentimental woman. She wants to remind me of my happiness, and she doesn't want me to know she has such a soft heart."

Romantic? Sentimental? Soft-hearted? Sara stared at Mrs. Stein, only slightly less surprised than she would have been if Mrs. Stein had just announced that Margaret was secretly Supergirl. Before she could say anything, the door to the apartment opened behind them.

"Hi!" Margaret said brightly. "Did I miss anything?"

Mrs. Stein brushed her finger across the tip of her nose and nodded her head significantly, moves that Sara remembered from the old movie, *The Sting*, and then raised her eyebrows in question. Without thinking, Sara nodded back, and both women turned to smile brightly at Margaret.

"Welcome back, dear. Your friend and I were just becoming better acquainted. Why don't you bring that bakery box right on over here."

CHAPTER SEVENTEEN

The Stockton Family Trust held their meetings in a beautiful downtown high-rise that presided majestically over the Seattle skyline. Sleekly modern, its angled walls echoing those of Paris' Louvre, the place had a sharp-edged feel to it. Margaret wasn't at all certain she liked it. She imagined that on the ever-present rainy days they enjoyed nine months out of the year in Seattle the expansive array of windows provided a welcome, if weak, natural light, but it didn't quite work for her. It felt drafty and overproduced in some way.

She was early, of course. Squarely on her lap was her presentation backup, the PowerPoint ready on her laptop. The board had given each of them, CoGS and the city, just ten minutes to summarize their final pitch to the board and Margaret planned to squeeze every second out of her chance.

By mutual agreement, she and Sara had agreed not to discuss the meeting or the Stockton Industries building. Every hour they spent together made Margaret feel, well, happy. Sara was relaxing and fun and exciting and thoughtful, so many things

Margaret felt as if she had been missing in her life. She still couldn't believe she was falling for Granola Girl, but what could she do? Maybe after today, they could talk about the future.

The stairway door burst open behind her. Had Sara taken the stairs?

To her shock, it wasn't Sara. It was Jeremy, who looked as if he had just run a marathon in his navy suit.

"Jeremy! They have an elevator, you know. It's the eleventh floor."

"Elevator," he gasped. "Loading something. Couldn't wait…"

"For heaven's sake, Jeremy, what's the problem? You could have called or texted me."

He shook his head and mutely thrust a handful of papers into her hand.

"What is this?" Margaret demanded.

He leaned over, hands on knees, panting. "Read."

"Jeremy, you're going to have to step up those cardiac workouts."

She opened the document and began to read. After the first scan, she sat back. She must have misread it. She went back again and read more carefully, focusing on the technical aspects and the conclusion. After she checked the date, she said, "Where did you get this? And more importantly, why the hell didn't I see this before?"

His face was beginning to resume its natural color.

"Daisy. She pulled it from the archives a few days ago, but she didn't realize it was important. I just saw it a few minutes ago. God, I'm so sorry, I didn't know."

"Didn't you? You know this looks a lot like a deliberate attempt at trying to make someone look very bad."

"Ms. Winters, I swear. I would never do that to you."

Margaret cocked her head at him.

"Wouldn't you? You know, Jeremy, a lot of things have been going awry lately. If I didn't know better, I would say you were after my job."

He straightened up and met her gaze, his own indignant. "Wait a minute. Of course I want your job. Didn't you want your boss's job? That's how government works. But I'm not going to get it by making you look bad. I'll do it by making you look good. You get promoted and I can move up."

Margaret blinked. She couldn't dispute the logic of that. In fact, that's exactly what she had done herself. "So what's going on with the missing files?"

He sighed deeply. "I didn't do it, but it's still all my fault. I kept thinking she would…"

Margaret caught on at long last. "Daisy," she said.

"Yeah."

"Good grief, Jeremy, she's an intern. Just fire her."

"I can't."

"Are you sleeping with her?"

The dismay on his face was profound. "Oh, God, no. She's my cousin. My mother insisted I get her the slot."

Well, that explained a few things. "I'm just going to make a guess here that urban planning is not her first choice of career."

He shook his head ruefully.

"Oh, no. That's my uncle's idea. She hates it. She's just not into files and organization. She's an artist, a really good one. But, as my uncle says, 'you can't make a living in the arts.'"

Margaret laughed.

"Oh, I think we might be able to help her with that. You go back to the office and tell Daisy I'll want to see her later today after the meeting. Meantime, try not to worry. And thanks for getting this to me."

He gestured to the paperwork in her hands. "What are you going to do about this?"

Margaret blew out a breath and checked her watch. Sara had to be on her way already, it was too late to reach her in her office. What was she going to do? Damn it. She really wished Sara had a cell phone! They desperately needed to have a private conversation before the board meeting started.

What *was* she going to do about this?

* * *

At exactly one minute before three p.m., a young man emerged from the board room and said, "Ms. Winter? The board is ready for you now."

Margaret stood, gathering her items. "Aren't we waiting for Ms. Chandler?"

"Oh, she's been here for a while. She was visiting with her godfather for a few minutes, just a chat."

Damn. This is not going to go well. How can I warn Sara? If I were in her place I'd suspect sneaky crap.

They were waiting for her, the five board members and Sara. The men were in dark suits, the women in brighter suits, and Sara was wearing what Margaret assumed was her most colorful dress, woven cotton in every color of the rainbow. She greeted Margaret with a smile which Margaret had trouble returning.

The documents in her hand were burning her palms. How was she going to do this?

"Ms. Chandler, Ms. Winter, thank you for joining us," Chairman Theodore McFall said. "As you know we've had a chance to review your voluminous submissions and considered the advantages and disadvantages of each proposal, both from the perspective of the Trust and generally for the city. We wanted to give you an opportunity to summarize your positions before the board takes a final vote. So we thought we would start with…"

Now or never.

Margaret said, "I'm so sorry to interrupt you, Chairman. Five minutes ago, my assistant handed me documents, which we just discovered in the property archives, which materially affect the decision the board must make. I wish we had located these much earlier, but I can't, in good conscience, proceed without informing you of this additional information."

Surprise from most, a delicate frown from the chairman, and a deeply puzzled look from Sara. Margaret risked a glance across the table to meet Sara's eyes.

I'm so sorry, she mouthed silently.

"This is an environmental report that was prepared a few years ago on the Stockton Industries Building. Apparently you were considering a sale at an earlier time?"

McFall nodded.

"Yes, it fell through. I don't remember seeing a report."

"It's somewhat lengthy, and I'll be happy to have copies made for everyone. But if you'll allow me to summarize…"

He waved a hand. "Go ahead."

Margaret cleared her throat. She couldn't look at Sara again. "When the Stockton Industries building was first constructed in the 1920s, it was heated by two oil-burning boilers. The fuel for these boilers was oil stored in three USTs—underground storage tanks—buried in the basement of the building. At some point—it's not clear from the report when, exactly—there was a major leak from one or more of the USTs."

Everyone looked a bit confused. Except when Margaret risked a glance now at Sara, she was the only one who seemed to understand.

"The ground is contaminated," Sara said flatly.

Margaret nodded slowly. She glanced down again at her notes, but she didn't need them. She simply needed an excuse to look away. "Yes, at the time of this report, the remediation costs were estimated to be several million dollars. It would be more now. This would have to be a major factor in determining the suitability of the site for a community garden."

McFall said, "Wouldn't the ground contamination also affect the use of the property for a new building?"

"To a limited extent only. For a fairly modest sum, the contaminated area can be encapsulated with concrete sufficiently to render it safe for a building site. We've run into this before a couple of times when rehabbing older buildings in the city. Comparative to the cost of the project itself, it's pretty minimal. Much less than the cost of the soil mitigation, which as you imagine involves massive excavation and infill and testing to insure soil safety."

McFall glanced around the room at his fellow board members. "Well, if accurate, this certainly is an important development we need to consider. Ms. Chandler, any response to this new information?"

Sara was staring at Margaret.

"No," she said flatly. "If the soil is contaminated, CoGS will be withdrawing its bid for the property, since we can't stand the expense of that degree of mitigation."

Margaret's stomach was twisted into a Gordian knot of anxiety. Sara looked more than defeated. She looked betrayed.

The board took a recess. Margaret assumed they were verifying the information she had given them, and she couldn't decide whether she wanted the report to be true or not. But in the end, the conclusion was as she might have predicted: Sara withdrew the CoGS bid and Pacific Rim was cleared to be the next major industry player in the Seattle business community.

Margaret had won.

"Sara!" She ran to catch up with her as Sara headed for the elevator. "Wait!"

Sara jabbed at the elevator button with a vehemence Margaret didn't know she possessed.

"You have to believe me, I only just learned about this," Margaret said. "I wanted to talk to you before the meeting, to warn you. You don't have a cell phone!"

"It doesn't matter now," Sara said. "It's over. You got what you wanted. It's done."

"You're just talking about the property, right? Not…us?"

Sara turned, her eyes blazing. "You lied to me. You ambushed me. I trusted you and you used me. Was this all just a seduction to keep me off balance?"

"Sara, you know that's not true!"

"I don't know anything of the kind. I hope your building project goes well. Please don't call my office again."

The elevator arrived. Sara stepped inside and warned Margaret with a glare not to join her.

"Goodbye, Margaret."

Margaret watched her own shattered reflection slide into place as the elevator doors closed and Sara disappeared.

CHAPTER EIGHTEEN

She did not need Sara Chandler. She didn't need Mrs. Stein next door. She didn't need anybody. Well, maybe she needed another glass of wine and the new romance novel on her bedside table, but that would have to wait until she got home.

What she did *not* need in any way, shape, or form was a phone call from her mother, but that's what she got.

"Honey, I haven't heard from you in a few days. How are we?"

"*We* are fine." Oh, she had never hated the royal "we" more than right now.

"You don't sound fine, dear. What's wrong?"

"Mother, I just closed the deal on the biggest project to hit downtown Seattle in years. It was the culmination of years of work and I'm exhausted. But happy."

"Dusty, I know when you're happy. This is not happy. Is it Sara? How is she? Are you two all right?"

Margaret sighed. "No, we are not all right. We are not 'we two' anymore."

"Oh! What happened? What did you do?"

"You know, Mother, it might not be my fault."

Silence on the other end of the phone contradicted her assertion.

"Look, Mother. She's making an unwarranted assumption about my motives and that's not my fault."

"It's not really about fault, Dusty. It's about reparation."

"What?"

"Blame is useless. It's focused on the past. You have to focus on the future. If you were wrong, say so and apologize. If she misunderstood something, then you need to explain it. What you can't do is just sit around feeling sorry for yourself."

Why not?

"It takes two to make a relationship, you know," Margaret said. "If she doesn't want to see me or talk to me, there's not a lot I can do about it. I'm not going to start stalking her."

Her mother snorted.

"Don't be ridiculous, Dusty. Have a conversation with her. Put yourself out there. Show her your true heart. If she rejects you after that, it wasn't meant to be. But you'll never have to wonder if you should have tried harder."

Great, even her mother was starting to make sense. How had the world turned upside down in such a short time?

All she had to do next was figure out how to track down Sara. Well, no. She had done that once already. So what she really needed to do was figure out if she really *wanted* to track her down. And what to say to her when she did.

Margaret stopped by Jeremy's desk on her way out. For the first time she could remember, he actually looked haggard, as if he had been nibbling at the now ragged edges of his goatee.

He looked up in surprise. "You're leaving early. You never leave early," he said.

"I am today. I sent you a letter I want you to print out and send to Daisy's father."

"Her father? Did you talk to her?" His eyes were wide, and his Adam's apple bobbed as he swallowed hard.

"We had a nice chat. I am telling her father what a hard worker she is and how ill-suited she is to this career. I have a recommendation for an excellent art program she can enter where I think she could be successful. I don't know if that will influence him, but we can try. She will not be returning to work here, by the way. I will expect that all my future requests for plats and files will be promptly met."

"Yes, Ms. Winter. And…thank you. For everything."

"You're welcome. I think we are going to accomplish some very good things in the future, Jeremy. Success for both of us."

CHAPTER NINETEEN

Margaret hesitated on the doorstep. She knew Sara was home. Even if the car visible in the garage hadn't given it away, she could see through the beveled windows in the door that the back door to the old barn-shaped home was wide open. Still, there had been no answer to her knock or the doorbell chimes. Frowning, Margaret pulled her phone from the pocket of her trousers and checked to be sure she hadn't missed a text. Or a call.

Nothing.

Of course there would be nothing. Sara had told her to lose her number.

Trying not to feel like a creeper, Margaret leaned closer to the door in an effort to see different areas of the room. Afternoon sunlight spilled through the back windows and open back door, warming the wood floors to a honey blond that contrasted with the rich dark wood framing the walls and built-in bookshelves. A worn Persian rug anchored the furniture in the room she could see, framed by the age-darkened wood beneath. Beautiful.

Peaceful. The space she could see just called out for a book, some tea, and relaxing.

Blowing out a breath, she considered her options. She had taken a gamble, simply hopping on a ferry and coming over. It was bad enough that she had gotten Sara's address by some creative sleuthing, but now here she was, peeking in her windows. Glancing over her shoulder, Margaret was grateful for the huge sequoias and thick underbrush that at least hid her from Sara's neighbors. Damn it, she really needed to see her, to talk to her, about last week's meeting!

Just a few short weeks ago she realized she would have snorted a cynical "of course!" after learning that Sara lived in a place called Dolphin Point. Not only that, but she lived off the very end of the trail, apparently the last house on the dirt road that extended past…civilization, it seemed. Now, of course, the location seemed absolutely right to her.

The house really did look like an old barn had been repurposed into a home and a large one at that. Beautiful old and weathered wood formed the sturdy structure, their lines interrupted by white-coated windows open to the warm afternoon breeze. The yard was free of trees immediately around the home, allowing anyone inside a clear view of the Sound and of Mt. Rainier in the distance. *A million-dollar view*, Margaret mused. She wondered how Sara's Peace Corps parents had managed it, then chastised herself. It wasn't really her business.

She peeked again through the windows. It was odd that the back door was open when it was clear nobody was here, and that made her nervous. You would think the stray, at least, would have come running when…come to think of it, when she had rung the doorbell there'd been no barking dog. Maybe Sara had gone for a walk? No, she wouldn't have left the door open, would she? Margaret ran a frustrated hand through her hair. Maybe she *couldn't* answer? What if they had gone for a walk and Sara had fallen? Seriously, the woman needs a damn phone! Maybe the dog was hurt? Maybe…maybe…

Christ, Margaret. You're going to "maybe" yourself into an early grave!

She stepped away from the door and made her way around the wraparound porch to the back. She was just going to check, she decided. Make sure there was nothing wrong. The slim, old boards creaked under her as she walked. Not alarmingly, but instead in that well-worn but still solid way that reminded her of her grandparents' old place. Margaret trailed her hand along the worn but recently revarnished rail, admiring the work that had gone into keeping the obviously old home in such great shape. Had Sara done the work? If so, the woman was really talented.

The side porch followed the shape of the house around to the back, revealing a sweet porch swing and opening into a sweeping covered porch draped with rich drooping purple flowers. She had no idea what the flowers were, but their scent was incredible and not overpowering. She stopped for a minute to simply inhale and...breathe.

A muffled "woof" made her focus again on her search. She stepped off the porch, appreciating the beauty of the yard and old-growth trees. Straight off the back of the deck the ground sloped downward, toward the Sound, though the treetops that were visible to her told her the path must drop a fair few feet to reach the water. To her right stood raised beds that had recently been cultivated and staked; the tiny shoots of what she imagined were tomatoes were already beginning their structured climb skyward. To the left of the deck, slung on two spectacular sequoias hung a hammock currently occupied by both Sara and the mutt. The dog's head was resting on Sara's stomach, but her eyes were focused on every move Margaret made. The tip of her tail flicked up and down, as she noted Margaret's attention.

Sara's voice was nearly a lazy drawl. "Unless you're Ed McMahon carrying balloons and an oversized check, I am not home."

Margaret continued to move forward, her low boots making soft sounds in the grass. She stopped in the shade of the tree and watched as the dog eyed her, never moving her chin from Sara's stomach.

Lucky dog.

She cleared her throat, then said, "I don't think it's Ed McMahon anymore."

"Be tough, since I'm pretty sure he's dead."

"Valid point." Margaret cleared her throat again. "Hey, I'm sorry to bother you at home."

"And yet, here you are." Sara's eyes were still closed, one hand rested on the dog's back, gently massaging the fur under her fingers. Her voice was soft but not warm in any sense of the word.

Margaret felt the distinct chill. Nope, this was a mistake. Whatever connection she thought she had with Sara, it was clear that Sara didn't, or hadn't, felt it as well. Or if she had, it hadn't been enough to withstand her disappointment and anger. "I should go." Margaret sighed. Coming here had been a bad idea.

"Margaret." Sara's voice was still quiet, but her eyes were open and fixed on Margaret's face. "You're here. What do you want?"

"I wanted to…" Margaret felt her frustration rise. "I needed to talk to you." She ran her fingers through her hair, a gesture she had long since trained herself from doing because it left her looking like a crazy person. "I warned you that this might happen, that things might get…sticky."

"Sticky." Sara echoed softly, her hand tightening on the dog's fur once before she loosened her fingers and patted Dusty's back. "Time to get up, girl."

Dusty's head popped up, and she waited while Sara got off the hammock, then she laid her head back down on her paws. It might be time for Sara to get up, but clearly Dusty was staying put. Sara's smile was faint as she rubbed her fingers over the top of the dog's head, "Fine, lazy girl, stay there." She turned to Margaret. "Come on." Without a word she turned and headed for the back porch. She waved a hand vaguely in the direction of the worn table and chairs and then disappeared into the house.

Margaret, with one last glance at the dog lounging in the hammock, stuck her hands in her pockets and stepped up onto the porch. She bit her lip and, deciding she'd pushed her luck far enough, seated herself instead of following Sara inside. Tucked neatly under the wooden trellis, the table was mostly in shade. A battered wicker basket slumped near the edge; a small three-pronged tool poked out of one side and a pair of worn leather gloves lay limply over the edge of the basket. Next to it lay a trowel, its bowl still caked with dirt from recent work.

After a long few moments, Sara returned with two full glasses, setting one before Margaret before taking a sip from her own and sitting in the opposite chair. She said nothing, merely raising an eyebrow. When Margaret said nothing, Sara rested her elbows on the table and reached for the trowel, tapping it against the edge of the table to loosen the dirt.

Margaret wasn't certain she liked the idea of having this conversation while Sara was armed. Still, she had come this far...

"Sara."

Sara glanced up before shoving the trowel into the basket and dusting off her hands.

"You are really lousy at following instructions," Sara said. "Which part of 'lose my number' did you not understand? You've called my office every day for a week."

"Didn't matter. You never answered."

"Margaret. Give it up. I have nothing to say to you. Clear enough?"

"Very clear. I'm here to ask you to give me two minutes. Two minutes, and then if you want me to leave, I will. And I will delete your number. You have my word."

Sara crossed her arms.

"Two minutes."

"No interrupting."

"I promise."

Margaret swiftly summarized what happened outside the board meeting. "I considered getting an affidavit from Jeremy, but you can call him. I had no idea what was going on and when I did learn it, there was no way to tell you, you were already inside the boardroom."

Sara opened her mouth, then closed it again, true to her word.

"I've spent the last week talking to Pacific Rim, and I think I have a plan that CoGS might find acceptable. But this isn't about the building. The plan is, I mean. But I'm not here about that."

Sara lifted an inquiring eyebrow.

"This is about us. I would never lie to you, Sara. I'm ambitious, yes, but I'm not ruthless. And you mean more to me than Pacific Rim ever could. I want to be with you, Sara. I want to take Dusty on long walks, and laugh about my mother's cheese, and sleep in with you on Saturday mornings. Can we try? Can you give us a chance?"

Sara was silent for a long moment. Finally she uncrossed her arms.

"I thought you lied to me. It hurt."

Oh, that shot hit the mark and Margaret winced. "I know. I—"

"No, it's my turn." Sara took another sip of her drink, her eyes on the glass. "You hurt me, but…that's on me. I mean, when I thought about it, I really couldn't believe that you would outright lie to me. Maybe bully a little bit to get your way, but after…well, after everything, I thought I knew you better. I did a lot of thinking this week and I don't know if I would have done anything differently if I had been in your shoes."

Margaret felt her heart lift a little, but Sara still wouldn't meet her gaze. She leaned forward, catching Sara's eye. Very slowly she reached out and pulled the glass from Sara's hand. Her fingers were damp from the sweat of the ice, but Margaret could feel the calluses under the skin. The solid strength in those hands. Her own fingers tightened as she took a firmer grip, her thumb caressing the back of Sara's fingers.

"Does this mean you're willing to give us another chance?"

Sara stared down at their joined hands for a long moment, and Margaret felt her heart sink. She looked so lost, so uncertain. Margaret tried again, "Sara, talk to me. What can I—"

"I have one condition," Sara interrupted.

Margaret's stomach flipped.

"What's that?"

"I need to know you're really all in."

"I am."

"I need to know...why your mother calls you Dusty."

Oh, God.

"You're serious."

"You know *my* full name."

"Well, yes, but...but that was just from backgrounders. From...okay, so I was curious." She rose and stepped around the table, Sara's hand still in hers. "And *your* first name is beautiful."

"You're trying to distract me. Are you in or out?"

Commitment comes in many forms, she thought. Taking a deep breath, she said, "It's my first name."

"Your first initial is S, not D."

Oh, this was going to be so much harder than she thought. "The 'S' is for...Stardust," she admitted softly.

"Stardust?" Sara gaped at her. "Your full name is...Stardust Margaret Winters?"

"Yes." She knew she probably looked pained as she added, "Can we not repeat that to anyone else?"

Sara threw her head back and laughed, then jumped to her feet. "That is perfect. Just perfect." Shaking her head, she grinned at Margaret. "I think I really love your mother."

Wrapping her arms around Sara, Margaret let herself sink into the embrace, burying her nose in Sara's hair. "Those are not really the words I want to hear right now, you know." Sara hugged her tightly and Margaret squeezed back. "But for now, they'll do."

CHAPTER TWENTY

A small crowd gathered near the front doors of the old Union Stables building in Seattle's historic Belltown district. Gone were the large, cumbersome, and forbidding old metal doors, the heavy lintels, the dark exterior so characteristic of the place. Tall glassed doors framed in warm brown wood and set under quartered windows filled the space that had once held heavy stable doors. Long, brushed nickel door handles that spanned the height of the glass doors provided a modern contrast, giving a hint of what was to be found inside. A long, green ribbon hung loosely between the handle on the far left door and the far right, waiting for the grand opening.

The building, just down the street from Sara's office and two blocks from the busy waters of Elliott Bay, rose five stories above the intersection of Western and Blanchard. Its red-bricked walls epitomized early 20th century neoclassical style. Hints of columns in the bricks that framed the windows ran from the ground floor to the top. The four centermost sections featured huge half-circle windows, mullioned like the rest of the building's. Centered between the high clerestory windows of the fifth floor was a large, circular medallion featuring a three-dimensional horse's head in three-quarter profile. To either side of the medallion the words "Union Stables" were carved in what Sara assumed was white marble inset into the brick façade.

Sara stood at the back of the small crowd and glanced at her watch. Margaret was running late. When she had asked Sara to attend this opening with her, she had told her she would meet Sara there, that she was coming straight from the office. Checking her watch again, Sara noticed a few photographers mingling with the crowd, as well as the local news van setting up across the street. Whatever opening this was, it was pulling in some solid media coverage.

"Excuse me." A broad-shouldered man apologized for bumping Sara from behind.

"No problem." Sara flashed a brief smile at him and then did a double take. A circular logo was embroidered on his polo shirt, with a stylized robot supplanting da Vinci's "Vitruvian Man," and the words "Pacific Rim Robotics" completing the circle around the robot. Looking around, Sara noticed others wearing the same logo on various articles of clothing.

She frowned, confused. In the ten months that she and Margaret had been dating, losing the bid to Pacific Rim Robotics because of her company's inability to financially support ground-water contamination remediation was still something of a sore point for Sara and they'd both made an effort to not mix work and their personal lives. Despite finding another suitable location for her first Community Garden project, Sara still felt a bit of a twinge when she thought about the original property and what its prime location could have meant to the locals. She had to admit, though, that the setback of losing that first bid for space due to environmental issues had led to good things.

"Hey. Sorry I'm late." Margaret appeared at Sara's elbow and gave her a quick kiss on the cheek, interrupting her train of thought.

"Hi." Sara searched Margaret's face; she was excited, her eyes alight. "What are the PRR people doing here? I thought they were—"

"Ladies and gentlemen, if you could all step forward." The announcement interrupted her. Before she could speak again, the announcer added, "Would Ms. Winters please join us on the platform?"

"Be right back," Margaret whispered as she kissed Sara's cheek again and slipped through the crowd.

Puzzled, Sara blew out a breath and waited for the program to start. A hand on her elbow made her turn, and she smiled as Margaret's mother reached out for a hug. "Carol! What a nice surprise. What're you doing here?"

Carol tipped her head toward the people sorting themselves out on the platform and smiled. "Margaret wanted me to come, so here I am."

"You don't come to all of these things, do you?" Sara's eyebrows drew together. "Do they *do* this sort of thing for every project she works on?"

"I have no idea. This is the first time she's asked me to come. Oh, they're starting." Carol lifted a finger to her lips as Margaret stepped to the microphone.

"Hi, everyone. Thanks for coming. I'm Margaret Winters, director of Neighborhood Development for the city. When CEO Kay Carney came to me looking for a Seattle home for Pacific Rim Robotics, she had some pretty specific criteria." Margaret exchanged glances with a distinguished-looking white-haired woman standing beside her. "Kay wanted modern, stylish, and accessible to local transportation. We have plenty of that here in Seattle. What we don't have, however, are a lot of places to build new that meet that criteria. Instead," she gestured to the building behind her, "we have a great many lovely historical buildings that need new life. And new life comes in many forms." Margaret's gaze flicked out over the crowd until she caught Sara's and then held there.

"Our first choice of site was a popular one, but as many of you know, we learned rather late in the bidding process that the land itself was unsafe for development, and unsuited for occupation. I reached out to Kay and then out to Jim Callahan, CEO of Grassroots Gardens, the parent company of Community

Gardens of Seattle, a local organization, and together we've come up with something that fulfills PRR's requirements and can further help our community."

Jim stepped out from behind the others on the platform and gave a brief nod to the assembled audience at Margaret's introduction.

Sara sucked in a breath. *What?* She looked from Carol to Margaret, then back again. "What?" she whispered. "But...I, nobody said anything to me. I don't—" She stopped, stunned. "That...that's Jim Callahan. But...he's in New York!"

"Clearly not, honey." Carol slipped an arm around Sara's waist and squeezed. "She's been working on this for months. Listen."

Margaret was still watching Sara as she continued. "I learned, recently, of how hard it is for people who live in the area to get fresh food, especially fresh vegetables. So, working with a representative from Community Gardens and with Kay, we developed a plan. I'll let Kay take over from here."

Margaret stepped aside as Kay Carney took the microphone. "Hi, everyone. When Margaret explained what was wrong with the first site and the impact any development would have not only for us but for the community, she proposed a few changes. One of the things we at PRR realize is that we cannot build and sustain new technology without respecting the past or taking care of our future. So, PRR purchased the original Pine Street property and will, in cooperation with the EPA, work to decontaminate the land. After its revitalization, we will build PRR's newest facility there, a robotics and technical training institute, with the space and capability to host rooftop community gardens.

"But"—Carney paused, her hand in the air—"we didn't want to wait for that process to be complete before moving our headquarters here to Seattle, and I, personally, hated the idea that a worthy community resource was not going to be available for a long time to come. So, together with the CoGS team, we retrofitted and repurposed this wonderful and historic building to not only suit our purposes but to also support the need for accessible community gardens for the wonderful citizens of Seattle, starting today. We also just learned this morning that, as of today, we've been awarded 'gold' status by the U.S. Green Building Council's Leadership in Energy & Environmental Design program."

Carney smiled as the crowd applauded. "Now, instead of talking about what we did, let's show you." She gestured to Margaret and Jim and the three of them took the oversized scissors someone handed them. Counting down, together they cut the ribbon and let it fall away. Cameras snapped and people applauded as the sparkling doors were pulled open and Kay stepped inside to begin the tour.

Sara and Carol stood back, waiting for the crowd to enter before them. When Margaret joined them, she had Jim in tow.

"Sara!" Jim Callahan enveloped her in a hug. "I'm so glad you're here!"

"Hey, Jim. I'm...well, I had no idea you and Margaret knew each other."

Jim grinned. "I know. It was a hard secret to keep. Even though you've been pretty buried with the Pioneer Square project."

Sara nodded, still reeling at learning her boss and Margaret had been working together for months.

"Jim, this is my mother, Carol. Mom, Jim Callahan."

Carol returned Jim's handshake, smiling up at him. "So, Jim. How about a tour?" She glanced over her shoulder at Margaret and gave her a wink as Jim nodded. "See you later, honey."

Margaret turned to Sara, her expression cautious. "So? Surprised?"

Sara could only stare at her. "You think?"

"Good surprise or bad?"

Sara studied her, considering. "Why didn't you tell me about this?"

Margaret blew out a breath. "At first, because we weren't sure we could get the whole thing going. There was the National Registry, then the building commission. And plans. Oh my god, the plan revisions. And Jim, wow. The man's a bit of a lunatic!" Margaret winced. "Sorry, but he is, you know."

She couldn't help but chuckle at that. "Well, yes. But for a good reason, right?"

Margaret took Sara's hand and led her toward the entrance. "Oh, you bet. He had so many *amazing* ideas! And when you put him and Kay in a room together, look out!" Margaret shook her head. "I think Kay's assistant took to bringing in two devices to make sure she captured all of the ideas. Anyway, once it was clear things were going to happen, I, um, asked Jim if we could make it a bit of a surprise."

"Oh, it is."

"Again, good surprise or bad?"

Sara smiled up at her. "I think it's a good one, really."

The smile that slid across Margaret's face lit her up, and Sara couldn't help but smile back. "Come on, sneaky. Show me what you did."

Margaret pulled her inside and Sara simply watched and listened. The place was immense. Large ten-inch square timbers spaced regularly around the room supported the open, timbered ceiling. Centered in the main lobby was a huge, open staircase, dark metal railings contrasting with the shining warm wood of the stairs and huge wooden beams. The squared logs, Sara realized as she got closer, were worn and dented, clearly part of the original structure.

"Look at this," Margaret said. "The building was built in 1909 and these were the original stalls. These beams have been here since then. I'm so glad we saved them. They said that during its heyday nearly three hundred horses were kept here during the day." Large, six-inch square posts showed wear from the hundreds of horses kept in the old stable and now framed workspaces with sleek design tables and computers. The lighting was cleverly done to not detract from the atmosphere. Reclaimed wood beams supported old pipes with a rich patina, the lights mimicking gas lamps.

Margaret continued the tour, pointing out historical things of interest here and there while Sara followed, absorbing it all.

When she would have gone up the staircase, however, Margaret pulled her back. Instead she led her to a small elevator set on the far side of the lobby. "Let's go this way."

Sara merely lifted an eyebrow but said nothing as they entered and Margaret pushed the button for the roof.

When the doors slid open, Margaret let go of her hand and waved Sara forward. Sara stepped out and simply stopped. The elevator doors had opened onto…a farm. There was no other word for it. Long, straight rows of plants, broken every sixty feet or so by a gravel path. The rows were in sections about forty feet wide, some with tall, wooden stakes already supporting tendrils of plant growth, others low and bushy, with small placards stuck into the rich, dark earth. Interspersed here and there were greenhouses, small seating areas, or low garden benches. The entire roof of the building, a structure that took up an entire city block of Seattle, was covered in abundant life.

Awestruck, Sara walked down the rows. A number of the plants had clearly been started elsewhere before being replanted here: the air was redolent with the rich scent of ripening tomatoes mixing with the moist, loamy smell of newly turned earth, all colored by the taste of sun-warmed greenery floating on air kissed by the nearby Sound. Sara stopped at the end of a row and found herself facing the water. The building offered a spectacular view of Elliott Bay and the Olympics, a better view than that in her own office. When Margaret stepped up behind her, Sara leaned back into her and simply enjoyed.

After a few moments Margaret spoke up. "Well?"

"Good surprise. Definitely."

"Good." Margaret turned her around and pointed out some things Sara had missed on her trip through the urban farm. "Those poles over there? They open and form a deployable sunshade system to control solar heat gain. It'll also keep a lot of the plants from getting too much sun, which, honestly, I didn't think was a problem here until Jim came on board."

"He's good at stuff like that."

"Yes, he is." Margaret kissed Sara's hand. "So, there's a party about to happen downstairs, want to go?"

"Do you?"

Margaret looked at her and then slowly shook her head. "Honestly? I would much rather just be with you."

"Then," Sara said, rising on her toes to give Margaret a quick kiss. "Let's get out of here."

EPILOGUE

The mountain glowed. There was no other word for it. It was a surprise to Sara, someone who had always thought of herself as a "sunset" kind of person, to realize just how happy she was that her home faced east. Instead of a nightly show—at least when the Pacific Northwest's weather cooperated—of a blazing sun painting the sky in brilliant shades of red and orange as it silhouetted the Olympic Range before dropping from sight, she was instead treated to this. The spectacular and stately Mount Tahoma, "Rainier" to the white settlers who "discovered" it, bathed in a nearly indescribable wash of color. Reddish-orange hues gilded the snow-covered cap and gradually changed tone as they flowed down the mountain to end in a deepening magenta-tinged purple, a shade echoed in the crags and shadows cast along the mountain's face. The depth of that glorious color was enhanced by the streaked mirror image floating on the nearly still waters of the lower Puget Sound. That same Sound's ever-present moisture added an otherworldly pearlessence, making it seem as if the very air were shimmering with color.

The silence around her was the silence of a rural evening, birds and insects, the far-off bark of a dog, the gentle lap of water on the shore. The air, as rich in the color suspended in its moisture as with the scent of the Sound and sea, carried within it a heady mix of grass, flowering apple trees, ripening blackberries, and so much more.

Taking a long, slow, deep breath in, Sara leaned back in the old porch swing, feeling as if she were inhaling the breath of the mountain herself. One leg dangled, her sneaker-clad foot giving the swing a gentle, controlled push; the other was folded beneath her. Beside her, Dusty lay stretched out, taking up the remaining two-thirds of the swing, her head resting on Sara's knee. Like Sara, the dog was relaxed, but her eyes were open, alert, and focused on the figure walking toward them. Her tail gave a little twitch and her golden-brown eyes moved from the approaching woman to her own Girl.

"Hey." Margaret's quiet voice did nothing to disturb the quiet mood. "Got room for one more there? I come bearing gifts." She held up two glasses of wine.

Sara nodded and patted Dusty's head. "Make room, big girl, go on."

Dusty let out a deep groan and reluctantly slid down from the swing, but not without sending Sara a reproachful look. She padded to the edge of the deck, circled once, and flopped down again with another groan, this time closing her eyes.

Margaret smiled as she settled onto the swing. "Why do I feel guilty?" she asked as she handed over a glass.

"Because that's what she wants." Taking a sip of the crisp white wine, Sara smiled. "Oh, perfect. Thanks." She turned to face Margaret and gently tapped the edge of her glass to Margaret's. "Congratulations."

"Back atcha." Margaret's smile deepened. She, too, took a sip and sat back on the swing, taking over the gentle movement when Sara pulled her other leg up and crossed it with her other, settling her back more comfortably. They sat together in silence, enjoying the play of sun and light and shadow. Even after the color began to fade, the mountain stood out in the deepening gray.

"I was thinking," Sara began. "You know, of what you said at the opening about new life, and more about why I wanted so much to come home. It's about roots, I think. I have them, of course, but spread all over. Nepal, India, South America, here...but, they're not deep. They never lasted." She tipped her head toward the steady, solid presence of the mountain resting against the horizon. "I want something that lasts, that'll root deep and grow."

Margaret nodded when Sara turned to her. "I meant what I said, that what we would build there was only the beginning." She reached out and pulled Sara's hand into her lap, her fingers playing gently with Sara's.

Sara gave Margaret's fingers a squeeze and kept her hand there, enjoying the feel of her hand in Margaret's. "I know. That's what I was thinking about." She looked again toward the mountain, disappearing into the darkness. "I like what we've built there, and...I would like to build that here. With you."

Margaret lifted Sara's hand to her lips and brushed a gentle kiss across the back, sending a shiver down Sara's spine. She gave in to the gentle tug and rested her head on Margaret's shoulder, letting out a long, slow breath. "Will you move out here, with me?"

"I was hoping you would ask. I can't really picture you in the city." She took another sip of her wine. "Though..." she paused long enough to have Sara tip her head back and look up to meet her gaze. "I don't suppose you would consider changing the dog's name, would you?"

Muffling a laugh in the soft curve of Margaret's neck, Sara stretched up to meet Margaret in a kiss. "Not a chance." She snuggled deeper into the curve of Margaret's embrace, inhaling the scent of her, of home. She was, indeed, home to stay.

Bella Books, Inc.

Women. Books. Even Better Together.

P.O. Box 10543
Tallahassee, FL 32302

Phone: 800-729-4992
www.bellabooks.com